THE MYSTERY OF TALLY-HO COTTAGE

The Twelfth Adventure of the Five
Find-Outers and Buster the Dog

The Mystery of Tally-Ho Cottage was first published in the U.K. in 1954 by Methuen & Co. Ltd. This edition was published in 1965 by May Fair Books Ltd. This impression was published by Wm. Collins Sons & Co. Ltd, 14 St. James's Place, London, S.W.1, and was printed in Great Britain by Love & Malcomson Ltd, Brighton Road, Redhill, Surrey, England.

ENID BLYTON

The Mystery of
Tally-Ho Cottage

COVER ILLUSTRATION
BY MARY GERNAT;
TEXT ILLUSTRATIONS
BY TREYER EVANS

ARMADA
PAPERBACKS
for Boys & Girls

"Why, Ern, did you really make it all yourself?"

AT PETERSWOOD STATION

ONE AFTERNOON four children and a dog walked into the little railway station at Peterswood. The dog ran about happily, his tail wagging all the time.

'Better put Buster on the lead,' said Pip. 'We're early, and two or three trains may come through. Here, Buster—come to heel, old boy!'

The little Scottie trotted up, his tail wagging nineteen to the dozen. He gave a few short barks.

'Yes, I know you're longing to see Fatty,' said Pip, bending over him to clip on his lead. 'So are we all! Hey, keep still!'

'Hang on to him—here comes a train!' said Larry. 'It's going right through.'

Buster stood his ground bravely until the train gave a piercing whistle as it tore through the station—then he tried to scuttle under a wooden seat and dragged Pip after him. He sat down with his back to the train and trembled. That awful whistle!

'It made *me* jump!' said Bets. 'Cheer up, Buster—Fatty will soon be here. We've loved having you while Fatty's been away, and you've been Very Very Good!'

'Even Mother likes you!' said Pip, patting him. 'Though she didn't a bit want us to keep you while Fatty was in Switzerland!'

'I can't think WHY Fatty had to go off to Switzerland for a whole fortnight, and be away all Christmas time,' complained Bets.

'Well, he had to go with his parents,' said Daisy. 'I expect he had a jolly good time in all that snow.'

'Yes. And he wouldn't mind falling down a bit, he's so plump!' said Larry, with a laugh. 'What's the time? Gosh, we're early! What shall we do?'

'It's cold on the platform. Let's go into the waiting-room,' said Daisy. 'Come on, Buster.'

Buster sat firm. Pip pulled on the lead. 'Come on, idiot. We're only going into the waiting-room. Fatty's train isn't due yet.'

Buster refused to move. Fatty was coming on one of the trains that clattered into the station, and would alight on this platform—and therefore Buster wished to wait there and nowhere else.

'Tie him up to the seat,' said Larry. 'He'll be miserable if we make him go into the waiting-room. Buster, you're an ass. I wouldn't sit down on that icy-cold stone platform for anything.'

They tied Buster to the seat and left him there. They went into the waiting-room, which had a very minute fire, but was at least sheltered from the cold wind that blew through the station.

'There's one thing,' said Daisy, sitting down on a hard wooden bench, 'Fatty won't be in disguise, so he can't trick us this time! He'll be arriving with his father and mother, and will have to be himself.'

'I'm glad,' said Bets. 'I want to see him just as he really is, fat and jolly and grinning all over his face! We haven't seen him for months! Three months at school— and then he rushes off to Switzerland!'

'I bet I know what he'll say as soon as he sees us,' said

Pip, grinning. 'He'll say, "Well—got any mystery on hand?"'

'And we haven't,' said Larry. 'Peterswood has been as good as gold. Goon can't have had anything to do at all!'

Goon, the village policeman, had indeed had a peaceful fortnight. Not even a dog had chased a sheep, and nothing as exciting as even a small burglary had happened. Goon had had plenty of time for snoozing in his big armchair!

A taxi drove up to the station, followed by a second one. A man leaned out of the window of the first one and beckoned to the one and only porter.

'Hey, porter! Come and take these cases. Look slippy, we've not got much time!'

The voice was loud and clear. The porter ran up at once, and took out two small cases. A man got out of the taxi and helped out a woman. Both were middle-aged, well-dressed and cheerful-looking. The woman carried a tiny white poodle.

'Darling Poppet!' she said. 'Don't get a cold in this icy wind!' She tucked the little thing under her fur coat and only its quaint little pointed nose looked out. The four children, watching from the window of the waiting-room, thought it was a little dear!

Four or five people got out of the second taxi, all rather hilarious. They had evidently come to see off the first two.

'Buck up, Bill—you've not got much time to get the tickets!' said the woman with the dog.

'Plenty of time,' said Bill, and strode into the station. 'Hallo—is that a train in the distance? My word, we'll have to hurry after all!'

The woman rushed on to the platform with the little dog. 'Oh, it isn't our train after all!' she said. 'It's going the other way. Oh, Poppet, what a shock I got!'

The new-comers made such a stir and commotion that the four children came out of the waiting-room to watch. Everyone was very hilarious.

'Well, be sure to have a good time!' said a red-haired

fellow and thumped the man called Bill on his back, so that he had a coughing-fit.

'Send us a telegram when you get there. We'll miss you and your parties!' said a woman.

The woman with the dog sat down on the seat to which Buster was tied, and set the little poodle down on the platform. At once Buster began to sniff at her woolly fur, and the little poodle yelped in sudden fright. Buster ran round to the front of the seat, twisting his lead across the woman's legs. She screamed and snatched Poppet up at once, afraid that Buster was going to take a snap at the poodle.

To make matters worse another train thundered into the station at that moment and Poppet nearly went mad with fright. She leapt out of her mistress's arms and tore off at top speed. Buster tried to race after her, forgetting all about his lead, and nearly strangled himself! He got caught up in the woman's legs, and she fell over, squealing loudly.

'Oh! Catch Poppet, someone! Oh, what's this dog doing? Get away, you brute!'

There was a terrific commotion. All four children tried to catch Poppet, and then Pip went to rescue poor Buster who was being well and truly kicked by the scared woman. She was very angry indeed.

'Whose dog is this? What do you want to tie him up under a seat for? Where's a policeman? Where's my dog?'

'Now now, Gloria, don't get upset,' said the man called Bill. Nobody took any notice of the train that had just come in, not even the four children. They were so concerned about Buster, and poor frightened Poppet!

So they didn't even notice Fatty stepping from the train with his father and mother—an extremely sunburnt Fatty, looking plump and the picture of health. He soon saw the others, and was rather astonished to find them so engrossed that they weren't even looking out for him!

'You get a taxi, Mother,' said Fatty. 'I'll walk back with the others. I see they're here.'

Fatty walked over to where Pip was trying to apologize to the angry woman and her husband. He now had his hand firmly on Buster's collar, and Buster was trying his hardest to squirm away. He began to bark loudly—and then suddenly wrenched himself from Pip's hand.

'Well!' said a familiar voice, 'at least SOMEbody recognizes me! Hallo, Buster!'

All the four swung round at once. Bets ran at Fatty, almost knocking him over. 'Fatty! You're here!'

'It looks like it!' said Fatty, and then there was a general clapping-of-backs and friendly punches. Buster nearly barked the station down, he was so excited. He pawed so hard at Fatty's legs that Fatty had to lift him up, and carry him!

'Whose dog is that?' demanded the man called Bill. 'I never saw such a badly behaved one in my life. Knocked my wife over, and made her coat all dusty! Ah—there's a policeman—come over here, my good man. I want to report this dog. It's been out of control, attacked my wife's poodle, and caused my wife to fall down!'

To the children's horror, there was Mr. Goon! He had come to buy a paper at the station, had heard the commotion, and walked on to the platform to see what it was. He still had his bicycle clips on his legs, and his bulging eyes gleamed with pleasure.

'Sir! This dog made a savage attack, you say! Just let me take down a note. Ah—this dog's been a pest for a long time—a very—long—time!'

Goon took out his notebook and licked his pencil. What a bit of luck to have a real complaint about that horrible dog!

The train pulled out of the station, but nobody noticed. Everyone was looking at the little group of children surrounded by grown-ups. Buster leapt out of Fatty's arms as soon as he saw Goon and danced joyfully round his ankles. Goon flapped at him with his notebook.

'Call this dog off! Here, you, call this dog off. I'll report him all right. I'll . . .'

Suddenly the woman gave a squeal of joy. 'Oh—here's Poppet back again—with Larkin. I thought you weren't going to come in time to take Poppet back home with you, Larkin!'

Larkin was a queer-looking fellow, who stooped as he walked, and dragged one leg behind him in a limp. He looked fat and shapeless in an old and voluminous overcoat, and had a scarf round the bottom part of his face and an old cap over his eyes. He carried Poppet in his arms.

'Who's this?' demanded Goon, looking with surprise at the queer fellow who suddenly appeared with Poppet.

'Oh, it's only Larkin, who lives in the cottage in the grounds of Tally-Ho, the house we rent,' said the woman. 'He was told to come to the station in time to collect Poppet and take her back again with him. He's going to look after her—but I *did* want to have my darling Poppet till the very last minute, didn't I, Poppet?'

She took Poppet into her arms and fondled her. She spoke to Larkin again. 'You'll look after her well, won't you? And remember all I told you to do. I'll soon be back to see to her. Take her now, before our train comes in and scares her.'

Larkin shuffled off, limping as he went. He hadn't said a word. Poppet had been handed back to him as if she were a doll, and was now snuggled into his coat again.

Goon was growing impatient. He still had his notebook in his hand. The children were wondering whether they could make a dash and go, but Goon had his eye on them.

'Now, Madam,' said Goon, 'about this dog here. Can I have your name and address, please, and . . .'

'Oh! Here's our train!' squealed the woman, and immediately everyone elbowed poor Goon aside and began to kiss and shake hands and shout out farewell messages. The man and woman climbed into a carriage and off went the train, with everyone waving madly.

'Gah!' said Goon, in disgust, and shut his notebook. He looked round for Buster and the others—but they were gone!

IT'S FUN TO BE TOGETHER AGAIN!

THE FIVE CHILDREN and Buster were halfway down the road, running at top speed!

'Good thing that train came in when it did!' panted Pip.

'Horrid old Goon! He *would* turn up just then!' said Bets. 'It wasn't Buster's fault. He wasn't doing any harm.'

'Let's hide somewhere till Goon's gone by,' said Daisy. 'He's got his bike, I expect, and he'll have a few nasty things to say to us if he sees us.'

'Oh yes, *do* let's hide,' said Bets, who really was very scared of the big policeman.

'Right. Here's an empty watchman's hut!' said Fatty, spotting it standing beside a place where the road was being repaired. 'Hop in. It will just about take us all. The back is towards where Goon will come from. He'll sail right by!'

They crowded into the little hut—only just in time! Goon turned the corner on his bicycle and came sailing

12

down the road at top speed, on the look-out for the Five—
and especially for that Pest of a Dog!

They all watched him sail past, his feet going rapidly
up and down on the pedals. They caught sight of his grim
face as he went by. Fatty grinned.

'There he goes. Well, we'd better keep out of his way
for a day or two,' he said. 'I expect he'll be after us about
old Buster. What *did* happen? Tell me. I was jolly surprised to find you all on the platform with your backs to
me, not caring tuppence whether I arrived or not!'

'Oh, Fatty—everything happened so quickly!' said Bets,
as they walked home with him. She told him all about tying
Buster up to the seat, and how the man and woman had
arrived with their friends, and how Poppet had got mixed
up with Buster.

'It was such a to-do!' said Pip. 'I'm awfully sorry about
it, Fatty—just as your train arrived too!'

'That's all right!' said Fatty. 'I was only pulling your
leg about it. Has Buster been good with you and Bets
while I've been away?'

'He's been angelic!' said Bets. 'I *shall* miss him. Mother
wouldn't let him sleep in my room or Pip's, as he does in
yours, Fatty—but he was *most* obedient, and only came
scratching at my door once in the middle of the night.'

'You're a very well-brought-up dog, aren't you, Buster?'
said Fatty, and the little Scottie danced in delight round
his ankles. 'Blow Goon! It was bad luck that he came up
at that minute. I bet he'll be after us for details of "Savage
Behaviour of Dog out of Control". I expect that's what he
wrote down in his notebook. We'll have to think what to
say to him.'

'Here we are,' said Pip, stopping by Fatty's gate. 'When
shall we see you again, Fatty? You'll have to go in and
unpack now, I suppose?'

'Yes,' said Fatty. 'Come round tomorrow to the shed
at the bottom of my garden. And if you see Goon just

say that as *I* own Buster, I'm the one for him to see. Well, so long! All news tomorrow! '

He went through the gate and round to the garden-door of his house. Bets sighed. 'Oh, I do wish we could all have had tea together or something. I'm just longing for a good talk with Fatty. Isn't he *brown*?'

Much to Bets' relief, Mr. Goon didn't appear at her home that day. When she and Pip set out the next morning to go to Fatty's shed, they both kept a good look-out for the fat policeman, but he didn't appear either on foot or on his bicycle.

Larry and Daisy were already down in the shed with Fatty. It was warm and cosy, for the oil-lamp was lighted and burning well. Fatty was just the same old Fatty, handing out bars of chocolate, and opening bottles of ginger-beer and lemonade. He grinned at Pip and Bets.

'Come on in. Seen old Goon?'

'No. Has anybody seen him?' asked Bets.

Nobody had. Buster went over to Bets and lay down beside her. 'He feels as if he belongs to you as well as to me, now,' said Fatty, smiling at Bets. He was very fond of little Bets, and she thought the world of Fatty.

'You *are* brown, Fatty!' said Bets, looking at his sun-burnt face. 'If you wanted to disguise yourself as an Indian or some other foreigner you'd easily pass for one.'

'Good idea!' said Fatty. 'I might try it on old Goon! I'm longing to get back to some real detective work again, and try out a few disguises. I don't get much chance at school—I only dressed up once last term.'

'What as?' asked Daisy, with a giggle. 'Go on—tell us. I know you want to!'

'It wasn't anything much,' said Fatty airily. 'Our French master fell ill and the Head had to send for a new one—and he—er—arrived early, and made a bit of a fool of himself.'

'Oh—did *you* pretend to be him?' said Pip. 'What did you do, Fatty? You really are a caution!'

14

'Well, I togged myself up, put on a moustache and those false teeth of mine,' said Fatty, 'and a wig of curly black hair, and a smile you could see a mile off because of the teeth . . .'

The others laughed. They knew Fatty's frightful false front teeth!

'Did you ask for the Head?' asked Bets.

'Gosh no—I'm not as fat-headed as all that!' said Fatty. 'I knew I'd find three or four of the masters watching the football that afternoon, so I made my way to them and talked to them very *earnestly* about the school. "And ze dear boys—zey await my coming, is it not? And ze—how you call him—ze Head—he awaits me also? Zis is ze football, is it not? Boom-boom—how zat boy kicked ze ball!"'

Fatty acted a Frenchman to the life, and the others roared at him. 'I don't think they liked me very much,' said Fatty. 'They all muttered something about classes and wandered off one by one. My teeth put them off, I suppose. They were jolly surprised when the *real* French master turned up!'

'What was he like? Anything like you pretended to be?' asked Larry.

'Not a bit. He was little and rather bald, and had a beard and teeth you'd hardly notice!' said Fatty. 'It all caused quite a commotion. A scare went round that the first man must have been someone who wanted to get in and rob the Head's safe—and the poor new man couldn't *think* why people were so surprised to see him.'

'I don't know how you dare to do such things,' said Pip. 'I'd *never* dare—and if I did I'd be found out at once. I can't think why you're hardly ever spotted, Fatty. There must be something about you—you do carry things off so well!'

Fatty looked pleased. 'Oh well—I've got to practise a bit if I'm going to be a real detective some day. Have some more ginger-beer? Now—have you found any mystery? A mystery would be just about the best news I could hear.'

'There's not been a sniff of one,' said Larry, drinking his ginger-beer. 'Goon must have been thoroughly bored this Christmas—I don't believe anything's happened at all.'

'Sad,' said Fatty. 'After two weeks of doing nothing but fall about in snow I did hope I could exercise my brains as soon as I got home.'

'Tell us about Switzerland,' said Bets. 'Did you really fall down much?'

It appeared that, far from falling down even once, Fatty had done extremely well in all forms of winter sport, and had carried off quite a few prizes. He tried to talk about them modestly, but, being Fatty, this was very difficult.

'Still the same old Fatty,' said Larry, after about twenty minutes of listening to Fatty's exploits. 'The Wonder Boy! Can't put a foot wrong even on skis!'

'Didn't stand on his head once!' said Pip, grinning. 'My cousin Ronald said he was more often upside-down than the right way up, when *he* went to the winter sports. But not our Fatty!'

'Don't tease him!' said Daisy. 'You'll stop his traveller's tales. He's got plenty more, haven't you, Fatty?'

'Well, *I* want to hear them, even if nobody else does!' said Bets, who never minded Fatty's boasting.

Fatty sighed heavily. 'Ah well—I don't want to bore you!' he said. 'You tell me *your* news. How many Christmas cards did you have? Was your turkey done to a turn? Did the fairy doll look nice at the top of your Christmas tree?'

'Shut up, Fatty,' said Pip, and gave him a punch. That was the signal for a general scrimmage in which Buster joined in delight. They were all shrieking so loudly that nobody heard a knock at the shed door. Buster was almost barking his head off, and he didn't hear it either.

The shed door opened, and Fatty's mother, Mrs. Trotteville, looked in. 'Frederick!' she called, in amazement.

'FREDERICK! Whatever is going on here? You'll have the oil-stove over. FREDERICK!'

Buster heard her first, and stopped barking. He stood and stared at her, and then gave a yelp as if to say 'Stop this fooling, everybody! Beware!'

Pip suddenly caught sight of Mrs. Trotteville and extricated himself from the heap of bodies on the floor. Fatty's was underneath, having been well and truly pummelled.

'Fatty!' said Pip, in Fatty's ear. 'Look out—danger!'

With a great heave Fatty sat up and looked round. He saw the open door and his mother standing in astonishment there. He smoothed back his hair and grinned.

'Oh—Mother! I didn't hear you, I can't think why!' said Fatty, politely. 'Do come in. Have a chocolate—or some lemonade? I think there's a drop left.'

'Don't be foolish, Frederick,' said his mother. 'Really, to see you behaving like this—you must all have gone mad! You'll certainly have that oil-stove over, and then the whole place will go up in flames.'

'I've got a bucket of water ready over there, Mother,' said Fatty. 'Honestly, you don't need to worry. We were only—well, actually we were so *pleased* to be together again that we—er—we . . .'

'I can't wait while you think up some silly explanation,' said Mrs. Trotteville impatiently. 'I just came to say that that policeman, Mr. Goon, is on the telephone and wants to speak to you. I do hope, Frederick, that you haven't upset him *already*. You only came back yesterday.'

Goon on the telephone! The Five looked at one another in dismay. That meant he was going to get after old Buster after all. Blow!

'All right. I'll go and speak to him,' said Fatty, getting up and brushing the dust off various parts of himself. 'Blow Goon! It's all right, Mother—don't look at me like that, there's a dear. I HAVEN'T DONE ANYTHING WRONG, truly I haven't.'

17

And off he went up the garden path and into the house, Mrs. Trotteville behind him, and Buster scampering along too.

The others looked at one another. Now what horrid things had Goon to say?

POPPET THE POODLE

MR. GOON was getting impatient. Why didn't that Toad of a Boy come to the telephone? He began to bellow into it at his end.

'Hallo! HALLO! Are you there? HALLO!'

When Fatty picked up the receiver he was almost deafened by Mr. Goon's yells. He shouted back.

'HALLO, HALLO, GOOD MORNING, HALLO, HALLO, HAL . . .'

This time it was Goon that was almost deafened. 'Ho—you've come at last, have you?' he said. 'What you yelling at me like that for?'

'Nothing. I just thought we were having a kind of shouting-match,' said Fatty, in a most polite voice.

Goon began to boil. Fatty always had a very bad effect on him. He spluttered into the telephone.

'Now then, you look here, and don't you . . .'

'Can't hear you properly,' said Fatty, in a most concerned voice. 'Mr. Goon, can you speak a little closer to the mouth-piece?'

'*No!*' roared the angry policeman, 'and just you look here, I . . .'

'Look where? Down the telephone, do you mean?' said Fatty inquiringly.

Poor Mr. Goon nearly flung down the telephone. He roared again. 'I want you to come down here to my house tomorrow morning at ten o'clock sharp,' he shouted. 'About that complaint, see? That dog's out of control, and well you know it.'

'There wasn't time for you to get a proper complaint,' said Fatty.

'Ho, I got enough to go on,' said Goon.

'Ho, you didn't,' said Fatty, exasperated.

'What's that you say?' bellowed Goon.

'Nothing of any importance,' said Fatty. 'Right—I'll be along tomorrow—with my witnesses—including Buster.'

'No—don't you bring that there pest of a dog!' cried Mr. Goon. But it was too late—Fatty had put down the receiver with a bang. Blow Goon!

He went to tell the others, and they listened gloomily.

'We'll all come with you,' said Bets loyally. 'And of course we'll take Buster. He's the defendant, isn't he?—is that what you call it?—and he ought to speak up for himself!'

'He'll speak all right!' said Pip. 'What a nuisance Goon is! We haven't got a great deal of the holiday left, and we don't want it messed up by Goon.'

'Let's go out for a walk,' said Fatty. 'The sun's out now, and I want to get the taste of Goon out of my mouth!'

They all laughed. 'You say such silly things!' said Daisy. 'Come on—let's go down to the river. There are some baby swans there, and the parents bring them to be fed. We'll take some bread.'

They put on hats and coats and went up the garden path to the kitchen door to ask for bread. The cook put it into a basket for them and they set off for the river.

They fed the swans and then wandered up the river-path, enjoying the pale January sun. The swans swam with them for some way, the little cygnets following behind. They came to a small gate that gave on to the river-path, and Bets looked over it idly.

Then she pulled at Fatty's arm. 'Look—isn't that exactly

like the dear little poodle we saw yesterday at the station—the one whose mistress made all the fuss about Buster?'

They all looked over the gate. 'No—I don't think it's the poodle,' said Pip, adding, in his usual brotherly way, 'you *always* jump to conclusions, Bets. Now I come to look more closely, it's not a *bit* like the poodle we saw. It's too big.'

An argument began. 'It's not too big—it's about the right size,' said Daisy.

'You girls have no idea of size,' said Larry loftily.

'I'll soon prove it, anyway,' said Bets suddenly, and she began to call loudly. 'Poppet! Poppet, are you Poppet? Here, Poppet!'

And the poodle straightway ran over to the gate, its stiff little tail wagging like a pendulum!

'There you are!' said Bets triumphantly. 'What did I tell you? Poppet, you're a darling! Fatty, isn't she sweet? She trots about as if she learns ballet-dancing!'

'So she does,' said Fatty, seeing exactly what Bets meant. 'At any moment now Poppet will rise on her toes and pirouette! Poppet, why did you cause all that upset with Buster?'

Poppet put her little pointed nose through the gate and sniffed at Buster, who sniffed back. He licked the tip of Poppet's nose, and Bets laughed.

'He likes her! I wonder if she's lonely without her mistress? I didn't much like the look of that man who took her back home, did you?'

'Well, I didn't like what I could *see* of him, which wasn't much,' said Fatty. 'I wonder where they live—in that cottage there, I suppose.'

A small, not very well-kept cottage stood at the side of the garden. Much further away rose a big house, probably the one that Poppet's master and mistress had left the day before. No smoke rose from its chimney, so presumably it was now empty. But smoke rose up from the chimneys of the little cottage steadily and thickly, and the five children immediately pictured the muffled-up man sitting hunched over a roaring fire.

Poppet wanted Buster to play with her. She pranced away from the gate, came back, and pranced away again, looking over her shoulder as if to say, 'Do come! I'd like a game with you!'

Buster scraped at the gate and whined. 'No, no, Buster,' said Fatty. 'You're already in enough trouble with Mr. Goon without getting into any more! We'd better go.'

They were just turning away when a voice came from the cottage. 'Poppet! 'Ere, Poppet. Where are you? You come along in!'

Poppet immediately disappeared into a bush to hide, and lay there quietly. The children watched in amusement.

'Where's that dog gone?' said the voice, and footsteps came down a path—limping, shuffling steps—and into view came the same man they had seen the day before, dressed in much the same way, except that now he had no scarf round his neck.

The children saw that he had a dirty-looking, unkempt beard and moustache, shaggy eyebrows and bits of grey-black hair sticking out from under his cap. He wore glasses with thick lenses, and seemed to be short-sighted as he peered here and there for the hidden dog.

'I bet you could dress up EXACTLY like that awful man,' whispered Bets in Fatty's ear. He turned and nodded, amused.

'Just what *I* was thinking!' he said. 'He'd be very easy to copy, shuffle and all!! Look at Poppet—she's not going to give herself away—she's lying as still as a mouse.'

'Poppet! Poppet! Where *is* that wretched dog!' said the man in an exasperated voice. 'Wait till I get you, I'll show you I mean what I ses! Slipping out like that! I won't half thrash you!'

Bets and Daisy looked horrified. What, thrash a little thing like Poppet? Surely the man couldn't mean it!

Another voice came on the clear wintry air. 'Bob Larkin!

22

Didn't I tell you to come to help me with them potatoes? You come in and do them!'

The man scowled. 'I'm just coming!' he said. 'I'm after this dratted dog! It's got out.'

'Oh my word—I hope as how that gate's shut!' cried the second voice. 'We'll get into trouble all right if anything happens to that precious dog!'

A woman now came into sight, very thin, wearing a draggled skirt and a dull red shawl wrapped tightly round her. Her hair was so extraordinary that the children gaped to see it. It was obviously a wig, mouse-colour and much too curly—and much too crooked!

'That's a wig,' muttered Daisy to Bets. 'Poor thing, I expect she's bald.'

The woman was not a very attractive sight, for, besides the wig, she wore dark glasses. She coughed now and again, and pulled a thick green scarf round her throat and chin. Then she sniffed loudly.

'Bob Larkin! You come on in. I'm not going to make my cold worse coming out here and yelling for you. You come on in!'

The man suddenly saw the little dog hiding in the bushes. He pounced on her and gripped her. She whined in sudden fear. The man shook her angrily.

'I'll teach you to slip out like this! I'll give you a real good lamming!'

'Here, hold on,' said Fatty, at once. 'She's only a little thing.'

The man swung round and peered short-sightedly at the watching children. He hadn't noticed them before. Buster gave a sudden growl.

The man looked hard at the little Scottie, then at the children again. 'Why—you're the kids whose dog caused all that rumpus yesterday!' he said. 'Mr. Goon's been round to see me about that. That dog of yours is going to get into trouble, see? Now you get off that gate and go away—and don't you start telling me what I'm to do!'

I'm in charge here, and I'll complain to that bobby if you make any trouble!'

This wasn't pleasant hearing. Bets felt frightened, and took hold of Buster's collar. Buster's nose was still sticking through the bars of the gate, and he growled when Bob Larkin took hold of Poppet's collar very roughly and dragged her up the garden.

'Yes—you'd like to go to Poppet's help as much as we would, Buster, old fellow,' said Fatty, frowning after the man. 'But you've got into enough trouble for the time being. I'm sorry that fellow recognized us.'

'I suppose he and Goon have cooked up a whole lot of complaints between them,' said Larry. 'Well, at least you know that Goon's been to see this Bob Larkin, and you won't be surprised when he tells you tomorrow!'

'What an unpleasant pair,' said Fatty, as they walked on. They suddenly heard dismal howls coming from the cottage and looked miserably at one another. Poppet must be getting her 'lamming'. Horrid old man!

Buster growled and ran back to the gate, pawing at it. 'Good old Buster!' said Pip. 'Sorry we can't let you do a bit of rescue work!'

They went back feeling rather subdued. An interview with Goon tomorrow—and an upset over a dear little dog like Poppet. Things didn't look too good! Even Fatty couldn't think of any jokes, and they parted with hardly a smile.

'Tomorrow at Goon's, at ten o'clock,' said Fatty, when they said good-bye.

'Right,' said the others, and went off looking extremely gloomy!

A SLIGHT VICTORY

FATTY'S MOTHER had already inquired why Mr. Goon had wanted him on the telephone. When he told her she looked vexed.

'How unfortunate! Who is this woman that Buster tripped up?'

'I don't know,' said Fatty. 'She and her husband appeared to be going off on some trip or other, and four or five of their friends came to see them off. They were pretty noisy. I think they live at that house called Tally-Ho down by the river—next to the Daniels. I don't know what their name is.'

'Oh—*those* people!' said his mother.

'You sound as if you know them, but don't want to!' said Fatty, amused.

'I know which people you mean, but I certainly don't have anything to do with them,' said Mrs. Trotteville. 'They have behaved very badly since they took Mrs. Peters' house while she went to America—giving silly parties, going out in boats at all hours of the night—and, so I hear, not paying their bills! Let me see—what is their name? Oh yes—Lorenzo, I think!'

'Well, it was they who complained to Goon about Buster,' said Fatty.

'I see,' said his mother. 'I heard they were rather fourth-rate film actors, both the man *and* the woman—but haven't had any film-work to do for some time. Anyway, my dear boy, if they have gone away, Goon can't make much of a complaint. He's just being unpleasant, I expect.'

'Well, I'm going now, Mother,' said Fatty. 'I hope I come home all in one piece—and I hope Buster leaves Goon all in one piece, too!'

'You do exaggerate so, Frederick!' said Mrs. Trotteville. 'Just be firm with that tiresome policeman, and don't take too much notice of what he says!'

'I won't,' said Fatty, feeling suddenly quite cheerful. 'Good-bye, Mother—I'll tell you what happens as soon as I get back.'

He set off on his bicycle, Buster in the basket. The others were already waiting for him outside Goon's house. Bets looked rather pale and Fatty squeezed her arm.

'Cheer up! We're going to have some fun. I've got a lot saved up to say to Goon.'

They went to Goon's front door and knocked on it. Rat-a-tatta-tat-tat-TAT!

There came the sound of slippered feet and the door opened. It was the woman who came to clean the house for Mr. Goon. She stared at them in surprise.

'We've come to see Mr. Goon,' said Fatty. 'He told us to be here at ten o'clock.'

'Did he now?' said the woman, looking as if she didn't quite know what to do. 'Well, he didn't say anything to me about that. He went out in a hurry like, about half an hour ago—maybe he'll be back soon.'

'We'll come in and wait, then,' said Fatty firmly. 'He said ten o'clock, and it's exactly ten now.'

A clock in Goon's office began to strike just as if it had heard what Fatty said. The woman motioned them into the hall.

26

'I'd better not put you into Mr. Goon's office,' she said. 'He's got private things in there—important things. I don't have to move so much as a sheet of paper if I dust in there.'

'We'll wait in the parlour then,' said Fatty, and they all marched into a musty, fusty little room full of the smell of pipe-smoke. 'Pooh—let's leave the door open. What a smell!'

'I'll be out in the garden hanging up the washing,' said the woman, 'but I'll hear Mr. Goon when he comes and tell him you're here.'

'Right,' said Fatty, and the woman disappeared. They looked round the room. There was a large photograph on the mantelpiece of Goon's mother and father and family. The five children went to look at it in delight.

'Pa Goon looks as fat as Goon is now,' said Larry. 'And oh *look*—this podge of a boy with eyes sticking out of his head must be Goon!'

They all chuckled at the sight of Goon as a boy. 'He's very like Ern,' said Bets, and, indeed, he was! Ern was one of Goon's nephews, who had once been to stay with him and had a most unpleasant time!

'I wonder what Ern's doing,' said Bets, remembering the admiration he had had for Fatty. 'He came to see you just before Christmas, Fatty, to give you a Christmas present he'd made you—and he almost burst into tears when he heard you were in Switzerland.'

'Poor Ern,' said Fatty. 'I've no doubt he'll turn up again with whatever it is. Hallo—is that Goon?'

It was—and judging by the heavy tramp of feet in the hall, there were two others with him. Fatty debated what to do. Should he go and announce himself? But if Goon had visitors, he wouldn't be too pleased to be interrupted.

'We'd better wait a bit,' he said to the others. 'Perhaps that woman will hear him and go and tell him we are waiting.'

'She's busy talking to the woman next door,' said Bets, looking out of the window. 'How they can understand

27

what the other is saying, I really don't know—they're both talking at once!'

Voices came from the office next to the room the children were sitting in. First they were fairly quiet, and then they became loud. The children heard various words, and at first took no notice.

Then a word came that made Fatty sit up. 'Lorenzo!' Now, where had he just recently heard that name? It certainly rang a bell!

'They've *got* to be traced!' said a voice that was not Goon's. 'Those Lorenzos are the ones we want, I'm sure. Get hold of anyone who knows anything about them. Get hold of their best friends here and ask questions, and . . .'

The voice fell and the next words could not be heard. Fatty listened in wonder. He remembered now where he had heard the name Lorenzo—his mother had said it was the name of the people who owned Poppet the little poodle.

'Funny!' thought Fatty, 'it sounds as if they've run into trouble. I hope they have—if so, old Goon won't bother about Buster!'

There was the sound of movement in the little office, and then footsteps. The visitors must be going!

'Well, good-bye, Goon,' said a voice. 'You'll have to get going on this—it's a big thing. Pity we've just missed those rascals! Find out what you can from the Larkins— they may be able to tell you something. If we can't get our hands on the Lorenzos, we might at least be able to get hold of that picture. So long!'

There was the tramp of feet to the front gate. Fatty sat still, feeling startled. Why—what was this going on? Something had unexpectedly cropped up, that was certain. A sudden feeling of excitement surged up in him—it might be a Mystery! Something was Up! Something had to be Found Out! He'd tackle Goon about it and get the Five Find-Outers on the job at once!

Bets was surprised to see Fatty's face suddenly go red

"What's all this?" thundered Mr. Goon

with excitement. She thought he was feeling nervous at having to meet Goon and she slipped her hand through his arm. Fatty never even noticed it! He was thinking so very hard. What *could* the Lorenzos have done? What was this 'picture'? He must find out, he must!

Goon came back from the front gate humming a tuneless song. He was evidently feeling pleased with life. He didn't go back into the office but walked straight into the parlour, not knowing that anyone was in it.

He stopped dead when he saw the five children there, Buster safely on Fatty's knee. Buster gave tongue at once and tried to leap off, but Fatty held on to his collar.

'What's all this?' thundered Mr. Goon. 'What are you here for?'

Fatty stood up. 'Well, you said ten o'clock, and it's now twenty past,' he said. 'Perhaps you're too busy with the Lorenzo case to see us now?'

Mr. Goon looked extremely startled. 'The—the Lorenzo case?' he said. 'What do you know about *that*?'

'Not much,' said Fatty honestly. 'We couldn't help overhearing a few things just now, that's all.'

Mr. Goon lost his temper. 'Oho! Listening with your ear to the keyhole, I suppose? Eavesdropping on the Law! There's a penalty for that kind of thing, Mister Snoopy, let me tell you that! How *dare* you listen to private matters?'

'I didn't. I couldn't help hearing,' said Fatty. 'We all heard a few things. Short of stopping up our ears we couldn't help but hear. As for listening at the keyhole, that's nonsense. Your door was wide open and you know it.'

'Now, none of your cheek,' said Goon, beginning to go purple. 'I remember now—I told you to come about this here Pest of a Dog of course. Yes—a serious complaint has been made, very serious.'

He took out his notebook and looked through it, while

the Five gazed at him. Larry, Daisy, Pip and Bets hadn't the remotest idea what Fatty had been talking about, of course, because they didn't know who or what these mysterious 'Lorenzos' were.

'I know that the Lorenzos made a kind of complaint yesterday,' said Fatty, 'and I know that you've been to see the Larkins, who are in charge of Poppet ... and ...'

'How do you know that?' almost shouted Mr. Goon. 'Snooping round—interfering—I can't get rid of you. You're a Toad of a Boy. I always said so! Now about this here dog of yours ...'

'If the Lorenzos have gone off and nobody knows where, any complaint they made is not likely to be of any use to you,' said Fatty scornfully. 'Hadn't you better forget about Buster, and concentrate on finding the Lorenzos—or the picture, whatever it is, Mr. Goon?'

Mr. Goon knew when he was beaten. He shut his notebook and began to bluster. 'Well, if there's anybody else makes a single complaint about that dog—a *single* complaint, I say—he'll soon learn what happens to dogs that are Out of Control. Time he did too. If ever there was a more aggravating dog—yes, and a more aggravating set of children, I'd like to hear of them.'

'I'll be sure to let you know if ever we do hear of any,' said Fatty, in his most courteous voice, the one that always drove poor Goon to fury. 'Well, I take it you don't need us any more—unless you'd like to tell us a bit about this new case, so that we might help you!'

'GAH!' said Mr. Goon furiously, and drove the Five out before him, Buster barking madly. They all went out of the front gate and Mr. Goon bellowed over it, almost shaking his fist at them.

'And if you try Interfering with the Law, and messing about in this case, and telling me Clues that aren't Clues, I'll come and tell your parents!' he shouted.

'Mr. Goon, Mr. Goon, you'll be had up for a Breach

of the Peace,' said Fatty solemnly. 'You're making every-one look out of their windows.'

Mr. Goon retreated hurriedly into his house, muttering fiercely. The children got on their bicycles and rode off.

'A slight victory to us, I think,' said Fatty happily. 'Buster, you can breathe again!'

NOT SO GOOD!

THE CHIEF TOPIC of conversation that day was the five children's interview with Goon. Larry, Pip, Daisy and Bets could hardly wait till they got to Fatty's shed to ask him what he meant about the Lorenzos.

'Who are they? How did you know about them?' demanded Larry.

'I didn't. But my mother happened to mention this morning that the people who owned Poppet were called the Lorenzos,' said Fatty. 'So when I heard the name spoken by that other policeman—or perhaps he was a sergeant by his manner to Goon—well, it just rang a bell, and I knew they were all talking about the people who made a complaint about Buster! '

'But what have they done—the Lorenzos, I mean?' asked Bets.

'I don't know any more than you do,' said Fatty. 'Except that they seem to have gone away just when the police wanted them for something. And there's something about a picture too. My mother told me that they didn't pay their bills, so perhaps the trouble is about *that*!'

'Is it going to be a mystery?' asked Pip.

'I hope so,' said Fatty cheerfully. 'And if it is, old Buster here led us to it—didn't you, Buster? You've got a nose for mysteries now, haven't you?'

'Wuff,' said Buster, thumping his tail on the floor of the shed. Fatty gave him a biscuit.

'Well, there you are—a small reward for leading us to a probable mystery,' he said. 'The trouble is, we don't know enough about it to set about solving it. I mean—we don't *really* know what the mystery *is*!'

'Ring up Superintendent Jenks and ask him,' suggested Larry.

Fatty shook his head. 'No. I don't somehow think he'd like it—and I'd have to tell him I overheard talk about it in Goon's house—and Goon would get into trouble for discussing things like that without first finding out if anyone was about. After all, for all he knew, that woman in the kitchen might have overheard every word!'

'Well—I don't see how we're to find out *anything*,' said Larry. 'Goon certainly won't let us in on it.'

They discussed the matter over and over again. Should they go and interview the old fellow called Bob Larkin and see if they could get anything out of him? No, because he was already annoyed with them, and anyway Goon had got to interview him—and anyway again they didn't know what to ask the old fellow!

'We're being silly,' said Fatty, at the end of the long discussion. 'We're trying to run before we can walk. Let's forget it now—and sleep on it tonight. Things may be clearer tomorrow morning.'

Fatty spoke the truth! Things were indeed much clearer the next morning! The Five Find-Outers knew as much about the Mystery as Goon did!

It was in all the papers, splashed across the headlines. *'Priceless old picture stolen from famous gallery.*

Thieves just escape the net of the police, leaving their dog behind. Police looking everywhere for the Lorenzos.'

Mrs. Trotteville was down to breakfast first, and saw the paper. She gave an exclamation. 'Why—the thieves are those Lorenzos! The ones that live next door to the Daniels. No wonder all Peterswood disliked them!'

Fatty came in at that moment, and his mother told him the news. 'The thieves were the people you told me about yesterday, Fatty—the Lorenzos. I told you how badly they behaved, and what wild parties they gave. They upset their neighbours the Daniels very much. See—they're in the news this morning—the police are after them. My goodness me—our Mr. Goon will be puffed up with importance over this. It's right under his nose!'

Fatty slid into his seat and took the paper, his eyes gleaming. Aha! If it was all in the papers it didn't matter about Goon not telling him anything. The Five Find-Outers could make their own plans, and get going themselves. What a thrill!

Fatty read and read! He forgot all about his breakfast, and never even saw his father come into the room.

'Good morning, Frederick,' said his father, and neatly took the paper from Fatty's hands. 'What about eating your bacon and egg? By the look of it, it's almost congealed on the plate!'

'So it is!' said Fatty, surprised. 'Well, it isn't often I don't get on with a meal. My word, Mother, this is a bit of excitement for dull old Peterswood, isn't it?'

'I hope it doesn't mean you're going to get mixed up with that aggravating policeman again,' said his father, pouring milk over his porridge. 'Actually, I should imagine that your friend, Superintendent Jenks, will send a good man down here to deal with anything that arises. I can't imagine that Moon—Coon—what's his name now—Goon —could tackle a big thing like this. That picture was priceless—worth at least fifty thousand pounds!'

'I shan't get mixed up with Goon,' said Fatty. 'It's

much more likely he'll get mixed up with *me*! Anyway, I think I'll ring up Superintendent Jenks and ask if I can do anything to help.'

'Well, he seems to think a lot of you, goodness knows why,' said Mr. Trotteville, 'and it does seem as if you have a few brains sometimes, Frederick. Now, for pity's sake eat up that horrible-looking mess on your plate.'

Fatty swallowed his breakfast, thinking hard. The telephone went just as he had finished it, and he rushed to answer it, quite sure it must be the Superintendent ringing up to ask his help!

But it wasn't. It was Larry, very excited.

'I say! Did you see the news in the paper? It *is* a mystery after all! Right under our noses. When are we going to get on to it?'

'I'm going to ring the Super,' said Fatty. 'We'll get on to it all right. I'll telephone you later. Ring Pip and Bets for me, will you?'

'Right, Chief!' said Larry, with a chuckle, and hung up. Peterswood was in the news! And he and the rest of the Find-Outers would soon be Right in the Middle of Something!

Fatty sat down and thought for a while. What should he tell the Superintendent? That he had seen the two Lorenzos on the station yesterday—but then, many people had. Should he ask if he could go and see the Larkins? He might be able to get something out of them that Goon couldn't. Anyway he was certain that he could do *some*thing.

He went to the telephone and asked for the number. It was engaged. He tried again in ten minutes. It was still engaged. The police wires were humming today in that district!

At last he got the number and asked for the Superintendent. 'It's Frederick Trotteville here,' said Fatty. 'He knows me.'

His name was passed through to the Chief's office

—and Fatty heard the Superintendent's voice, sharp and impatient.

'Yes, Frederick? What is it?'

'Sir, it's about the Lorenzos,' said Fatty. 'As it's right where I live, can I do anything?'

'I fear not,' said the Chief. 'The Lorenzos are not there—and I doubt if the missing picture is, either. If they could be found, they would be found together!'

'Oh,' said Fatty, in disappointment. 'Then—isn't there anything I can do, sir?'

'Nothing—except keep your eyes and ears open as usual,' said the Chief. 'I'm sending a man down to go over the house with a tooth-comb, just in case the picture's there—but I've no real hope of it.'

'Will Mr. Goon be working on the case, sir?' asked Fatty, rather forlornly.

'Yes—but there isn't much case at Peterswood to work on,' said the Superintendent. 'I wish Goon had kept his eye on the Lorenzos more—they've a shocking reputation, as everyone knows!'

'I suppose I couldn't go and talk to the Larkins, sir, could I?' asked Fatty, feeling that this mystery was slipping out of his hands altogether!

'No. Certainly not,' said the Chief at once. 'My man is doing that, with Goon. No sense in your butting in there —you'll do more harm than good. I don't mean that you mustn't pass the time of day with them if you meet them— but you must remember that this case has really left Peterswood now—and gone goodness knows where! I don't for one moment think that the Larkins can possibly know anything that will be of the slightest help to us.'

'I expect you're right, sir,' said Fatty, feeling very down in the dumps indeed. 'Well, I won't keep you, sir. Good luck!'

He put down the receiver and looked gloomily at Buster, who was sitting nearby, with cocked ears.

'No go, Buster,' he said dolefully. 'It's all come to nothing. The mystery has fled from Peterswood and disappeared. Now I must telephone to the others.'

The other four were most disappointed. 'Oh, Fatty!' said Daisy, 'there must be *some*thing we can do! There really must. Come along up here to us, and we'll get Pip and Bets too, and talk about it. You *do* sound miserable!'

So they all met at Larry's at half-past eleven and sat down to a mid-morning snack of hot buns from the oven and cups of cocoa. They felt more cheerful after a couple of buns each.

'The Chief really did seem to think we can't do a thing this time,' said Fatty. 'Apparently the two main things are—*one*, to find the Lorenzos, who are probably out of the country by now—and *two*, to find the picture. And the Chief thinks that where one is, the other will be there also.'

'Well, we can't possibly go gallivanting all over the country looking for them ourselves,' said Daisy. 'So we must just be content to do nothing.'

'I think we might keep a watch on the house, perhaps?' said Larry. 'Just in *case* the Lorenzos come back to it.'

'They won't,' said Fatty.

'But what about their little dog?' said Bets. 'Mrs. Lorenzo really did seem attached to it—she might send for that, mightn't she? If it suddenly disappears we'd know that the Lorenzos had sent a messenger of some sort for it.'

'That certainly is a point,' said Fatty. 'Yes—perhaps on the whole, we won't give this up straightaway. But the thing is—how on earth are we to keep a watch on the Larkins to *see* if any messenger is ever sent? I mean—the house is some way from where we live, and we can't spend all our days—or nights—there!'

'Hopeless,' said Pip, who didn't particularly want to spend any part of a cold day or night watching people like the Larkins. 'We can't do it. If we knew somebody who lived next door, it would be easy—but we don't, so . . .'

'Hallo!' said a voice, suddenly interrupting, and a tousled head peeped round the door. 'I've been to your house, Fatty, and your mother sent me here. I've brought the Christmas present I made you!'

'ERN!' cried everyone. And sure enough it *was* Ern, plump as ever and red in the face. Good old Ern!

THE SAME OLD ERN!

ERN CAME right into the room, beaming, and holding rather a large parcel.

'Still the same old Ern!' said Fatty, and solemnly shook hands with him. Ern thereupon felt that he must shake hands with everyone, even Buster. Buster was very pleased indeed to see Ern, and leapt on him as if he were a long-lost friend.

'This is an unexpected pleasure,' said Fatty. 'How are your twin brothers, Sid and Perce? We haven't seen them since we all solved the Mystery of the Vanished Prince—do you remember?'

'Coo, yes,' said Ern. 'That wasn't half a do! I enjoyed that, I did. Perce is all right, as far as I know. I don't seem to notice him much. Sid's all right too.'

Sid had been a great toffee-sucker, unable to speak at all at one time because of the toffee glueing up his mouth! Bets remembered and giggled.

'Does he still suck toffee?' she asked.

'Well, he rationed himself up to Christmas, because he wanted to save money to buy presents,' said Ern. 'But then everyone went and gave him tins of toffee, of course, and he's off again. Can't get a word out of him now.'

'Except "Ar", I suppose?' said Pip. 'He used to say "Ar" quite a lot, I remember.'

'Yes. Well, he still says it,' said Ern. 'He isn't much of a talker, old Sid.'

'Sit down and have a bun,' said Daisy. 'What's in that parcel?'

'Coo, I was almost forgetting,' said Ern, beaming round again. 'It's something I made for you, Fatty. We did carpentry at school last term, and I said to myself—"Ah, Ern —this is where we do something for Fatty!" And I made *this*!'

He pulled off the paper and showed Fatty a small table, plain and simple. He had polished it till it shone.

Everyone exclaimed in surprise. 'Why, *Ern*!' said Bets, amazed, 'did you really make it all yourself?'

'Never let anyone touch it but meself!' said Ern proudly.

Fatty examined it from every side. 'It's a masterpiece,' he said. 'A beautiful piece of work. Thanks, Ern. I like it very much.'

Ern was bright red with delight. 'No kidding?' he said. 'You *do* like it?'

'I tell you, it's a masterpiece,' said Fatty. 'First-rate! We'll have it in my shed at home so that we can all see it and use it as much as possible.'

Ern was quite overcome. He swallowed once or twice, rubbed his sleeve over the table-top to make quite sure it was perfect, and then beamed at everyone again.

'Nice to see you all again,' he announced, sitting down. 'Anything on? Any mysteries going? I heard about them people called Lorenzos. Proper set-up, that was! I bet my uncle Goon's excited!'

'Have you seen him yet?' asked Daisy.

'Oooh no!' said Ern, in horror. 'I'd run a mile if I saw him. I'm scared stiff of him—he'd box my ears as soon as look at me! I kept a good look-out for him this morning, I can tell you.'

They discussed the Lorenzo case, and how maddening it was that the most important things concerned—the Lorenzos themselves and the picture—had both gone.

'So, you see, there's nothing much we can do, Ern,' said Fatty. 'I can't see anything we can get hold of—no clues or suspects, like we usually do.'

'Yes, it's bad luck,' said Ern sympathetically. 'I was hoping I might be able to help a bit, if you really wanted me. I'm coming to stay in Peterswood. My Mum's got to go to hospital for a bit—she's got a bad leg, poor Mum—so us kids are going to relations and friends for a week.'

'Good gracious—you're not staying with Mr. Goon again, are you?' said Bets.

'You bet I'm not!' said Ern. 'When my Mum suggested it, I fell off my chair in fright. Straight I did. I got this bruise, see?'

Ern proudly displayed a large bruise just on the point of going yellow and green.

'What did your Mum say then?' asked Pip. The Five were always interested in the doings of Ern's large family.

'She said, "All right, Ducks, I'll think of someone else,"' said Ern. 'And she did.'

'Who was it she thought of?' asked Bets. 'Anyone we know?'

'I don't reckon so,' said Ern. 'It's my father's cousin—a Mrs. Woosh.'

'What a wonderful name!' said Daisy.

They all tried it over. 'Woosh! Mrs. Woosh. Whooooooosh!'

'Sounds as if her husband ought to make rockets,' said Larry, and everyone laughed.

'Where does your Auntie Woosh live?' asked Bets.

'She's in the cottage belonging to a Mrs. Daniels, who lives at High Chimneys,' said Ern. 'Her husband is the gardener, and she helps in the house. She's got twins—girls they are, about the same age as Sid and Perce.'

Ern stopped when he saw the sudden, intense interest

on Fatty's face, at the mention of the Daniels. He looked at Fatty in surprise.

'What's up?' he said. 'You look all sort of worked up, Fatty.'

'I am,' said Fatty. 'I'm all of a dither, as our cook says when she falls over Buster. The Daniels! Did I *really* hear you say the Daniels, Ern?'

'Yes,' said Ern puzzled. 'What's wrong with that?'

'Nothing,' said Fatty. 'It's perfect. It's too good to be true! Don't you know that the Daniels live next to the house that the Lorenzos rented, Ern? And we wanted to keep a watch on it, but it's a good way from our own homes—and . . .'

'COO!' said Ern, light dawning on him suddenly. 'You mean—I say, do you mean I can come into this because I'll be able to pop my head over the hedge and watch any goings-on at the house next door?'

'You've got it, Ern!' said Fatty, and clapped him on the back. 'We were almost on the point of giving up the mystery when you came in—now we'll be on it full-speed! WHAT a bit of luck that you'll be staying with the Wooshes!'

Ern was so overcome that he was speechless for a moment. He stared round with bright eyes, and opened and shut his mouth like a goldfish.

He suddenly found his voice. 'I'll do my bit,' he said, in a suddenly solemn voice, just as if he were going off to war. 'You just give me my orders, Fatty—and I'll obey!'

Thereupon a most animated conversation began. The newspapers were fetched from downstairs, and everyone pored over the reports of the Lorenzo case. The Five Find-Outers meant to get every single bit of information they could find.

'It even says here that they left Poppet the poodle behind,' said Bets. 'And here's a picture of her in Mrs. Lorenzo's arms. And listen, it says: "Gloria Lorenzo is passionately attached to her little poodle, whom she has

43

had for seven years. It is the first time she has ever left the little dog behind—and therefore it seems that the Lorenzos meant to flee the country." '

'Ern could keep an eye on those awful Larkins, too,' said Daisy, 'and see that they don't ill-treat dear little Poppet.'

'I'll keep an eye on them,' promised Ern. 'You just give me my orders! '

'He could keep an eye on Tally-Ho, the house, as well,' said Larry. 'Just in *case* the picture has been left behind, hidden there somewhere after all. If he sees any suspicious strangers about, he'd have to report to us at once.'

'Yes, I will,' said the excited Ern. 'I'll have my bike, see—and I'll keep it all pumped up and ready to fly off to Fatty's if I've anything to report.'

They talked and talked. It was all most exciting. Ern's face grew redder and redder and his hair became more and more tousled. He had never had such a thrilling morning in his life!

'I expect old Goon will be round there quite a bit,' said Fatty. 'He'll keep an eye on the Larkins, and on the house too. So look out for him.'

'Lovaduck! ' said Ern, suddenly doleful. 'I forgot about my uncle. I'd better keep out of his sight. He'll go mad if he sees me snooping around.'

'He certainly will,' agreed Fatty. 'Don't let him know you're staying at the Wooshes if you can help it. Don't let him see you at all, in fact! '

'Oh, I won't,' said Ern fervently. 'I'm scared of my uncle, I really am, sure as my name's Ern Goon.'

Buster gave a sudden growl when he heard the name of Goon. 'There! ' said Ern, 'he thinks the same as me. Good old Buster. I know how you feel about biting his ankles. I'd like to bite him too.'

Buster thumped his tail on the floor, and looked at Ern with approval.

'I say,' said Pip, 'how old are those twins of your aunt's? About Sid and Perce's age did you say? You could have a game of ball with them, perhaps—and let the ball go into Tally-Ho gardens—and slip over and look for it—or . . .'

'Coo yes—I'll be able to think of plenty of excuses for slipping into next door,' said Ern. 'I'll pry into every corner —you never know where that picture might be hid, do you!'

'Well, it probably wouldn't be in the rubbish-heap or in the coal-cellar,' said Fatty gravely. 'I wouldn't bother about the picture, Ern—just keep your eyes and ears open and report anything unusual to us—strangers about, or noises in the night, or lights.'

'Yes—and report to us if the Larkins are cruel to little Poppet!' said Bets. 'If they are I'll get the R.S.P.C.A. to report them. I will. I really will!'

'Good old Bets,' said Fatty. 'Don't worry—the dog is a valuable one and the Larkins won't dare to starve it or hurt it badly.'

'I say—just *look* at the time!' said Pip, in horror. 'We'll be late for our dinner again—and mother will blame *you*, Fatty, as well as us! Come on, Bets, for goodness' sake!'

Larry and Daisy came to the front gate to see them off. They all rode away on their bicycles, Ern too.

'So long!' he said, with his usual beaming smile. 'I'm off to the Wooshes now. They're expecting me for dinner. I've got all my things in my bike-basket!'

'So long!' said Fatty, amused at the tiny bundle in Ern's basket. Ern obviously didn't think he needed much luggage for a week's stay at the Wooshes! 'And thanks most awfully for the splendid table, Ern.'

Ern rode off, pleased at the sight of Fatty riding away on his bicycle with the table under one arm. He'd be able to tell those twins something, when he got to his aunt's!

ERN HAS AN IDEA

ERN ARRIVED late at his aunt's, having quite forgotten that his uncle, the Daniels' gardener, knocked off work at half-past twelve and went in for his dinner.

Mrs. Woosh was not too pleased with him. 'Oh—here you are at last, Ern!' she said. 'Well, we've almost finished dinner—and thinking you weren't coming, Liz and Glad have eaten your share of the stew.'

'Oh!' said Ern, dismayed, for he was very hungry indeed. 'Sorry I'm late, Aunt. I've been with my friends and forgot the time.'

'What friends?' asked his aunt, in surprise.

'Well, there's Frederick Trotteville, and the Hiltons and . . .' began Ern proudly.

Liz and Glad tittered. 'Oooh, isn't he *grand*!' said Liz. 'Those aren't his friends, are they, Mum?'

'You hold your tongue, Liz,' said Mrs. Woosh. Liz nudged Glad and they both went off into giggles that made Ern long to slap them.

'If you were my sisters,' he began, glaring at them, but Mrs. Woosh stopped him.

'Now, Ern, don't start throwing your weight about as

his wife can't get in. Not even to air the house. He says the police have got the keys.'

Ern decided this might be important, so he wrote down 'Shut house. Keys.' His aunt frowned.

'Why do you keep scribbling in that notebook of yours, Ern, when I'm talking to you? That's rude. Anyone would think you were your uncle, P.C. Goon—he's always got a notebook he's scribbling in. My word, I've just thought of an idea!'

'What?' said Ern, his pencil poised over his notebook at once. 'Quick, Aunt!'

'I'll ask Mr. Goon in to tea while you're here—I'll tell him it's just so he can see his nephew. But really it'll be because I want to hear what he's got to say on this Lorenzo business!' Mrs. Woosh looked delighted at her idea. 'He's a wonderful man, your Uncle Theophilus Goon—always on to something. Yes, I'll ask him to tea.'

Ern stared at her in the utmost horror. He could think of nothing worse than having his uncle to tea, and being made to sit opposite his big, angry face. Why, he didn't even want his uncle to *know* he was in Peterswood.

'Please, Auntie, don't ask him,' begged Ern. 'He—well, he isn't very fond of me. I'm right down scared of him.'

'Oh, go on with you!' said Mrs. Woosh. 'He's not a bad fellow. I always say it's useful to have a policeman in the family.'

Ern didn't think so. He could have done without Mr. Goon in his own family, that was certain! He put away his notebook gloomily. What a pity it had reminded Mrs. Woosh of his uncle!

'Well, I'd better wash up, I suppose,' said Mrs. Woosh. 'You go on out and play with Glad and Liz, Ern. You'll get on with them fine!'

Ern wasn't so sure that he would. He put on his coat and went out. He was immediately pelted with bits of earth, and greeted with squeals of laughter. He looked round to see where the twins were. Up in that tree!

Ern was about to shout at them, when he stopped. The

tree was a tall one. It stood by the hedge, and overlooked the Larkins' cottage and garden. It would, in fact, be a perfectly splendid spying-place!

Ern decided not to be angry about the clod-throwing. He called up the tree. 'Hey, you kids! Like me to show you how to build a house in a tree?'

There was a moment's silence. Then Glad looked down cautiously. 'Yes. But don't you try lamming us when you come up. We'll push you down, if you do.'

Ern immediately felt like 'lamming' them. But he must keep guard on his temper. The twins might come in very useful!

The tree was some kind of evergreen fir, very tall and broad. Its branches were admirable for climbing. Ern went up to where the twins sat. They grinned at him.

'Did we hit you with the clods of earth? We waited and waited for you. Did Mum talk to you all that time?'

As the twins never really expected any answers to their questions they didn't at all mind when Ern ignored them, and began to make a peep-hole through the thick branches, so that he might look down on the Larkins' cottage over the hedge.

'What are you doing? Are you going to make a house up here? Can we live in it? Will it have a chimney?'

Ern found that he could see right down into the Larkins' garden—in fact, the cottage was so near that he could smell the smoke from the chimney. He took out his knife and began to cut away some of the greenery, so that he could have a kind of window through the branches to peep from. The twins watched him with interest.

'What are you doing? Is that a spy-hole? Can we spy on the Larkins? We don't like them. Let's throw a stone down their chimney!'

The last idea appealed to Ern very much. He had never tried throwing stones down a chimney, but it certainly looked quite easy from where he sat. Then he reluctantly dismissed the idea from his mind. No—he might be lucky enough to get one stone down the chimney, but there would be a dozen stones that missed—and they would rattle on the tiles and bring out the Larkins in fury. That would never do!

'Now you listen to me,' said Ern, taking command firmly. 'We'll play that the Larkins are our enemies, see? And we'll play that we've got to keep a watch on them and all they do. So we'll build a little house up here, and I'll keep watch.'

'Us too!' said the twins, both together. Ern nodded.

'All of us—when I'm not up here, you two can take a turn—and you'll have to report to me, see, because I'm your chief. This is our hidey-hole!'

The twins were thrilled. They gazed at Ern in admiration. He was clearly much, much cleverer than he looked.

'I'll go down and see if there's any bits of wood and stuff to bring up here,' said Ern, and disappeared rapidly. He stood at the bottom and called up cautiously. 'Now, keep watch while I'm gone, you two!'

He met his uncle as he walked back to the cottage. Uncle Woosh was a tall, silent man who only came into the house for meals and for very little else. Ern was rather afraid of him, but decided that his uncle was the man to ask about planks and nails.

'Yes. Get what you want out of my shed,' said his uncle. 'Plenty there.' He took himself off, and Ern ran to the shed, pleased.

Now to build a little place up in that tree—what a fine spy-hole! What would Fatty say to *that*!

ERN KEEPS WATCH

Two DAYS went by. Fatty and the others pored over the papers each day, but there was no more news of the Lorenzos, except that the police seemed more or less certain that they were hiding somewhere in the country, waiting to fly out as soon as things had quietened down a little.

'I should have thought that it would be very difficult to hide *any*where, with everyone on the look-out for you,' said Daisy. 'I mean—the Lorenzos would be very easy to recognize—their photographs have been in every single paper!'

'You forget that they have been actors,' said Fatty. 'It would be easy for them to disguise themselves so that nobody would know them.'

'Yes. I forgot that,' said Daisy. 'After all—if anyone was after *you*, Fatty, you'd be able to disguise yourself so that nobody in the world would recognize you!'

'Like you do sometimes now,' said Bets. 'Oh, Fatty— things are a bit dull at present—can't you disguise yourself? You know—dress up as an Indian or something. You do look so very very brown with all that dazzling Swiss sun—you'd pass anywhere for a foreigner. Go on— just for a bit of fun!'

'I'll think about it,' said Fatty, making up his mind that he would certainly do a bit of disguising, as Bets suggested, and have a little fun. 'By the way—I wonder how Ern is getting on. We haven't seen anything of him for two days.'

Ern had been getting on well. He now had the twins almost eating out of his hands—in fact, they were quite embarrassing in their hero-worship, and followed Ern about whenever they could.

He had made the house in the tree. Ern was very good with his hands, and thoroughly enjoyed taking charge of the proceedings, ordering the twins about, and showing off his clever carpentering.

Even his Uncle Woosh had taken an interest, and had helped Ern considerably. His aunt thought it was a lot of silly nonsense.

'Messing about up trees!' she said. 'Getting filthy dirty. Just look at the state the twins are in, after being up there all the morning!'

Their father looked at them and made one of his rare remarks. 'Can't see a mite of difference in them,' he said. 'They're always dirty.'

He walked out, followed by a string of exasperated remarks from his wife. Ern followed him.

'Women!' said Mr. Woosh, with a backward jerk of his head towards the cottage. 'Women!'

Ern nodded understandingly. Once his uncle had discovered that Ern, like himself, was interested in carpentry, he had been very friendly. Ern was quite enjoying his stay, especially now that the twins were so completely under his thumb.

The house in the tree was finished. It was quite an elaborate affair, and made of good strong planks securely fastened down. There were three walls and a very peculiar roof, that had to fit under some rather awkward branches. The missing wall, of course, was the 'spy-hole' that looked through the branches down on to the Larkins.

The twins' mother gave them some cups and plates, and allowed them to have snacks up in the tree. The twins were too thrilled for words, and were ready to do anything in the world that Ern told them.

Ern felt as excited as his two cousins. He had never imagined that it would be so easy to build a house up a tree. Of course, his uncle had helped a lot. Ern had to admit that.

He and the twins sat up there continually—but Ern preferred it when he was quite alone. There was something very thrilling indeed about sitting up in the thickly-leafed evergreen, in his own little tree-house, peering quietly through the opening he had cut in the greenery.

The Larkins had no idea that they were being spied on by three children. To the twins, of course, it was merely a game, like Red Indians—but to Ern it was serious. He was helping Fatty. He might be able to gather a few clues for him. He might see something suspicious—he might even help to solve the Lorenzo mystery! Though Ern had to admit to himself that that wasn't *very* likely!

He peered down at the Larkins' cottage whenever he could, watching for any sign of movement. He had supplied himself with a tin of bull's-eye peppermints, enormous things that bulged out his cheek, but lasted for a very long time. He also had a comic that he read at intervals, and he really thoroughly enjoyed himself, sucking away at his bull's-eye, hidden in the little tree-house he had built.

'Old Man Larkin doesn't do much!' Ern thought. 'Just goes out and picks some sprouts—and does some shopping—and lets the dog out and yells for it to come back. Poor little dog—it looks down in the dumps all right, and I'm not surprised!'

Certainly Mr. Larkin didn't appear to do very much work. As for Mrs. Larkin, she hardly appeared at all. Apparently she had a bad cold, and Ern could often hear her coughing. Once when she ventured out for a minute or two, to hang up some washing, Ern could hear her sniffing all the time. Sniff, sniff! Cough! Sniff, sniff!

She groaned as she bent down to pick up her washing-basket. Ern watched her, thinking she was a very ugly woman with her extraordinary wig of hair, and her very white face and red nose.

Poppet came out with her, her stiff little tail down. She kept well out of Mrs. Larkin's reach. The woman spoke to her in a hoarse voice. 'Don't you dare run off, or I'll lam you again, nuisance that you are!'

Poppet slunk into the house, and Mrs. Larkin followed, sniffing. Ern scribbled down a few notes about her in his notebook. He had torn out the notes he had made when his aunt had chattered to him, because when he examined them afterwards, such words as 'Donkeys' years', 'legs', 'midnight bathing' didn't make any sense to him.

But, sitting in peace up the tree, he could write quite sensibly. 'She sniffs and coughs,' he had written down. 'She wears a wig. Her voice is hoarse and croaky. Poppet is afraid of her. She groans when she picks things up.'

After two days had gone by, Ern decided that it would be a good idea to go and see Fatty and the others again, so off he went, notebook in pocket.

He found all the Five, with Buster, down in Fatty's shed, playing a game of cards. They were very pleased to see him.

Buster welcomed him at the top of his bark. Ern felt pleased to see that the table he had made for Fatty was standing in the middle of the shed, with a plate of chocolate biscuits on its polished top. He stood and grinned.

'Come in, Ern. Make yourself at home,' said Fatty, gathering up the cards. 'We've just finished our game. What's your news?'

'Well, I haven't much,' said Ern. 'Except that I've got a house up in a tree that looks right down on the Larkins' cottage, and into the grounds of Tally-Ho. I sit there and watch like anything.'

'Is it *really* a house in a tree?' said Bets, thrilled. 'Oh, I *would* like to see it! Ern, you *are* clever!'

Ern blushed. He drew out his notebook, and gave it to

Fatty. 'I've made a few notes,' he said. 'Not that they're worth anything—but you never know!'

Fatty glanced through them rapidly, and handed back the notebook. 'Very good,' he said. 'You're doing well, Ern. Yes, those might come in useful sometime—if only we could get going!'

Ern was pleased. 'You got anything interesting to tell me?' he asked.

'Nothing,' said Fatty dismally. 'It's too maddening to have something like this under our noses, so to speak, and not be able to get even a bite at it!'

'The only thing that's new was in the paper this morning,' said Larry.

'What?' asked Ern, who hadn't seen a paper.

'Well, the Lorenzos were spotted somewhere up north,' said Larry. 'Near an airfield, in a small hotel. And what is more they had a crate with them this time, as well as two small suitcases.'

'Coo—the picture!' said Ern. 'Weren't they caught then? Did they get away?'

'Yes—fled in the night—took someone else's car out of the garage and went,' said Fatty. 'Complete with suitcases and crate. I don't somehow think they will try to get out of the country at present. They'll hide somewhere safe and wait.'

'Would they come back to Peterswood?' asked Ern, thrilled. 'I'd better keep a strict watch from my tree-house.'

'They might,' said Fatty. 'And, as we said before, they might send someone to fetch Poppet, so keep a watch for any stranger at the Larkins' cottage, Ern, and keep a watch too to see that the poodle is always there.'

'Oh, I will!' said Ern.

He spent a pleasant morning with the others, and then, remembering that his dinner was at half-past twelve, not one o'clock, he rose to go.

'I'll be along again sometime,' he said. 'Good-bye, all. Thanks for the biscuits. Good-bye, Buster!'

Buster came with him as far as the gate, and saw him

off politely, his tail wagging fast. He liked Ern. Ern mounted his bicycle and rode off at top speed. He rang his bell going round the corner just at the same moment as somebody else rang theirs. Ern swung round the corner, pedalling furiously—to meet his uncle, Mr. Goon, also pedalling furiously on his bicycle! Mr. Goon, unfortunately, had cut the corner and was on his wrong side. The bicycles were about to crash together, when Ern quickly swerved. His pedal caught Mr. Goon's, and over they both went.

'Oooh! Oh!' groaned Mr. Goon, as he landed very heavily indeed. His bicycle fell on top of him.

'Oooh!' yelled Ern, and he too fell to the ground. He sent a terrified glance at Mr. Goon and got up. Mr. Goon groaned again. Then he saw who the other cyclist was, and stared open-mouthed.

'What! *You*, Ern! How dare you ride at sixty miles an hour round a corner! How . . .'

'It wasn't my fault, Uncle,' said poor Ern, scared stiff. 'You were on your wrong side.'

'I was not!' said Mr. Goon, most untruthfully. 'Do you mean to say you're accusing me of causing this here accident? You just wait, young Ern! What you doing in Peterswood, anyhow?'

Ern was not prepared to tell him that. He put his foot on the left pedal, and was about to swing his leg over to sit on the saddle, when his uncle gave a really most alarming groan.

'Oh, my back! It's broken! Here, young Ern, you help me up, come on, now!' He held out an enormous hand to Ern. 'Come on—give me a pull!'

Ern put out his hand too—but saw the gleam in Goon's eye just in time. He snatched back his hand and jumped on his bicycle, panting hard. Coo—his uncle had *almost* got him!

MR. HOHO-HA

Ern cycled back to his aunt's at top speed, turning round every now and again to see if Goon was after him. But mercifully there was no sign of his uncle.

It took Goon quite a minute to heave himself to his feet, and examine his bicycle to see if it could be ridden in safety. It appeared to be all right. Goon knew that it was no good trying to chase Ern. Indeed, if he did, Ern would certainly win!

Goon said a lot of things under his breath. 'That Ern! Wait till I get him! I'll pull all his hair out! I'll box every ear he's got! Why, he might have killed me. Speed fiend, that's what he is! What's he doing in Peterswood, I'd like to know!'

Goon had no idea that Ern was staying in Peterswood —and certainly none at all that he was living next door to the Lorenzos' house. He got on his bicycle very very carefully, fearful that something might be broken and give way beneath his weight.

He wondered what Fatty was doing. He hadn't seen or heard of him since the morning that all the Five had visited him. He began to scowl.

That fat boy was too cunning for words. Was he hoping to do something about the Lorenzo Mystery? Had he gone to see the Larkins and got out of them more than he, Goon, had managed to get? Was he working out something? Mr. Goon began to worry. He pedalled back to his house, still frowning.

'I think I'll go up to the cottage at Tally-Ho House and pop in to see the Larkins again,' he thought. 'I'll ask Bob Larkin if that fat boy has been snooping round—and if he has I'll have Something to Say about it.'

But Fatty had not been to see the Larkins because the Superintendent had said that he did not wish him to. Fatty was still rather down in the dumps, though he kept a cheerful face with the others.

He thought about Ern's rough notes, and wondered how little Poppet was getting on. In his notes Ern had put that she was afraid of Mrs. Larkin. She was terrified of Mr. Larkin too, so her life couldn't be a very happy one. After seven years of love and fuss and petting, life must seem very grim to little Poppet these days!

'I'm sure Mrs. Lorenzo will try to get her dog back, if she can't get out of the country,' said Fatty to himself. 'Or she will send someone to fetch her, and put her in a home with kindly people. I think it wouldn't be a bad idea if I went to see Ern's tree-house this afternoon, and did a bit of snooping round myself.'

He sat and thought a little more. 'Better not go as myself in case I bump into Goon. I'll disguise myself— I'll be an Indian, as Bets suggested!'

He looked at himself in the mirror, and twisted a face-towel over his head like a turban. Bets was right—he looked exactly like a brown-faced Indian! Fatty grinned and felt much more cheerful.

'It doesn't suit me to sit and do nothing when there's something on,' he said. 'That's not the way to make anything happen! Come on, Fatty—stir yourself. Get out your fancy clothes and dress up!'

Immediately after he had had lunch, Fatty set to work down in his shed. He found a fine strip of gay cloth that would do for a turban, and looked up 'Turbans—how to wear', in a very useful little book called *Dress up Properly*. He practised turban-tying for some time and at last produced a most satisfactory one, wound correctly round his head.

He pencilled a faint black moustache, rather thin, on his upper lip, and darkened his chin to make it seem as if he had a shaved beard. He put cheek-pads in to alter the shape of his face, and at once looked older, and fatter in the cheeks. He darkened his eyebrows and made them thicker, then gazed at himself in the glass, putting on a sinister, rather mysterious expression.

'That's all right,' he thought. 'Gosh, it's queer looking at myself in the mirror and seeing somebody quite different! Now, what else shall I wear?'

He decided that the Eastern clothes he had were a bit too gay for January weather. He didn't want a crowd of kids following him around! He suddenly thought of some Eastern students he had seen in London.

'They wore turbans, and rather tightish, but ordinary black trousers, and an overcoat,' he remembered. 'Didn't want to shiver in our cold climate, I suppose! Perhaps it would be best if I just wore a turban, and ordinary clothes. My face is so very sunburnt that just wearing a turban makes me look Eastern!'

He found a pair of rather dirty, very tight black trousers, which he couldn't do up at the waist. He had a brain-wave and tied a sash round his middle instead. Then he put on an old overcoat.

'A foreign student from somewhere out east!' he said to himself. 'Yes—that's what I am! Come on, Fatty—off to Tally-Ho!'

He left Buster behind, much to the little Scottie's dismay, and set off, passing rapidly by the kitchen window, hoping that the maids would not see him. But his mother saw him, and gazed after him in surprise.

'Who's that?' she wondered. 'A friend of Frederick's, I suppose. What a peculiar-looking fellow in that gay turban!'

Mr. Larkin jumped violently and dropped his wood.

Fatty went off down to the river, and made his way along the river-path. He only met an old lady with a dog, and she gazed at him uneasily. Was he going to snatch her handbag? But he passed quickly, and she heaved a sigh of relief.

Fatty came to the river-gate leading into the grounds of Tally-Ho. It was only a small wicket-gate, quite unlike the two imposing drive-gates at the front of the big house, through which so many cars had driven in and out that summer.

Nobody was about at all. Fatty went a little way along and climbed over the fence into the grounds. He made his way cautiously to the big house, standing, desolate and empty, with no smoke coming from its many chimneys.

He peeped into a window. Inside was a big room, with dust-sheets over the chairs. A large, polished table stood in the middle. On it was a great bowl full of dead flowers.

Fatty's gaze slid round the room. Chairs. Little tables. A stool—and lying on the floor beside the stool was a curious little object, grey, solid, and rubbery.

Fatty wondered what it was. And why was it on the floor? He stared at it curiously. Then he suddenly knew what it was. Of course! It was a little rubber bone, the kind given to dogs to play with and chew!

'Must be Poppet's,' said Fatty. 'One of her playthings that she left behind on the floor.'

He left the window and went along a path under a rose pergola—and suddenly, just at the end of it, he came face to face with Mr. Larkin, who was trudging round the corner with some firewood.

Mr. Larkin jumped violently and dropped all his wood. Fatty stepped forward at once and picked it up. Then he addressed the scared Mr. Larkin in a very foreign-sounding voice indeed!

'Excuse, please! I come here to see my old friends, the Lorenzos—ah, such old friends they are! And I find the house shut tight—nowhere is there anybody. Please, good sir, you can tell me of my friends?'

'They've gorn,' said Mr. Larkin. 'Ain't you seen the papers? Bad lot, they are.'

'Gorn?' echoed Fatty, in a very puzzled voice. 'I do not understand.'

'Well—they've gorn—just *gorn*,' said Mr. Larkin impatiently. Fatty stared at him. He looked just the same miserable old fellow as before—plumpish under his untidy old overcoat, a scarf round his chin and throat, and a cap pulled down over his eyes. He peered at Fatty suspiciously through his thick glasses.

'We don't allow no strangers here,' said Mr. Larkin, backing away from Fatty's stare. Fatty was taking him all in, suddenly filled with a longing to disguise himself like this old fellow. If he disguised himself as Bob Larkin he could go all round the house and peep into every window without anyone being surprised. He might even get into the house if he could find the keys. Possibly Larkin had some. Yes—he would do it one night—it would be fun.

'You'll have to give me your name,' said Mr. Larkin, suddenly remembering that the police had asked him to take the name of anyone coming to the house. 'Foreigner, aren't you?' He took out a dirty little notebook and sucked a pencil.

'You can write down my name as Mr. Hoho-Ha,' said Fatty politely, and spelt it out carefully for Mr. Larkin. 'And my address is Bong Castle, India.'

Mr. Larkin laboriously wrote it all down, placing his notebook on a window-ledge to write legibly. When he looked up again, Mr. Hoho-Ha had gone.

Larkin grunted and picked up his firewood. All this silly police business annoyed him. Why couldn't he be left in peace to do his job? But he didn't seem to have much of a job now! All those boilers raked out—nothing to light or keep going. No nice warm boiler-house to sit in and read his paper. Nothing to do but look after a silly little poodle!

Fatty was behind a bush, watching Larkin going down the path. He noted every action—the shuffling limp, the stoop, the way the cap was pulled half-sideways over the man's face. Yes—he could disguise himself well enough as Larkin to deceive even his old wife!

Fatty had a good look round while he was about it. He looked into shed and greenhouses, boiler-house and summer-house, keeping a sharp look-out for anyone else. But he saw nobody.

He would, however, have seen somebody if he had been near the Larkins' cottage! He would have seen Mr. Goon! Mr. Goon had ridden up to have another talk to the Larkins, and he was at that moment trying his hardest to get something out of Mrs. Larkin besides coughs, groans and sniffles.

Fatty would also have seen two other people if he had looked up into the tall fir-tree that grew beside the hedge which separated Tally-Ho grounds from the grounds of High Chimneys next door. He would have seen Glad and Liz!

They, faithful to their trust, had been on guard in the tree for two hours, while Ern was mending his bike. Ern's brakes had gone wrong, owing to his crash with Mr. Goon, and he wanted to put them right.

'Glad and Liz, you sit up there and keep your eyes open,' he said. 'And here's two bull's-eyes each to keep you going.'

Glad spotted the strange foreigner as soon as he climbed over the fence. She was so surprised that she swallowed the bull's-eye she was sucking and choked so violently that she nearly fell out of the tree-house.

When at last she recovered, the foreigner had disappeared. She found that Liz had spotted him too, and the twins gazed at each other in excitement.

'He must still be there!' said Glad. 'Come on, Liz—let's climb down and tell Ern. He'll go after him all right. Won't he be pleased with us!'

ERN SHADOWS A SUSPECT!

GLAD AND LIZ almost fell down the tree in their hurry. They went into the little shed where Ern was busy with his bicycle.

'Ern! We've seen somebody,' said Glad, in a penetrating whisper that could be heard all over the garden. Ern looked up, startled.

'Where? Who?' he asked, getting up at once.

Glad and Liz told him, and Ern straightway made for the hedge, and disappeared through it. He went cautiously round the Larkins' cottage—and then stopped in horror. Mr. Goon was standing at the door talking to Mrs. Larkin! The twins had not seen him because he had arrived after they had climbed down the tree.

Mr. Goon caught sight of Ern at the same moment that Ern caught sight of him. He couldn't believe his eyes. Ern again! Ern here in the Larkins' garden!

Mr. Goon gave such a roar that Mrs. Larkin disappeared indoors immediately and shut the door with a slam. Ern was too petrified to move. Mr. Goon advanced on him majestically.

'*You* here!' said Goon. 'Now you just come-alonga me, Ern. I've a few things to say to you, I have.'

C

Ern fled just in time. He ran blindly down the path and charged full-tilt into Mr. Larkin, who was shuffling along still carrying his firewood. He dropped it for the second time as Ern ran straight into him and almost knocked him over. He caught hold of the boy and held on—and was then almost sent flying by the burly form of Mr. Goon chasing after Ern.

''Ere! What's all this!' said Mr. Larkin, startled and annoyed.

'Hold that boy!' commanded Mr. Goon breathlessly. 'Hold him!' Mr. Larkin tried to hold the wriggling Ern, but had to let him go—and Mr. Goon just pounced in time to stop poor Ern from escaping. He shook him so hard that Ern didn't quite know what was happening.

'What you doing here?' demanded Mr. Goon angrily. 'Is that fat boy here too, snooping round?'

'No,' said Ern, feeling certain that Fatty and the others were playing some nice, friendly game far away in Fatty's shed.

'Mr. Goon, sir,' said Mr. Larkin, 'there's bin a furriner wandering round Tally-Ho grounds just now. Name of Hoho-Ha.'

'Why didn't you tell me?' said Mr. Goon unfairly. 'Standing there saying nothing. Where *is* the fellow?'

He hung on to Ern so tightly that the boy groaned. 'Uncle, let me go. I'm after him too. I'll look for him, if you'll let me go.'

'What do you mean, you're after him too?' said Mr. Goon, looking all round as if he thought he would be able to see plenty of 'furriners'.

'You let that boy look for him, sir,' suggested Mr. Larkin from under his old cap. 'A kid can snoop round quietly and not be seen. You're too big for that. You let this boy loose and tell him to find that furriner— yes, and follow him for you till you can catch up and nab him!'

Goon gave Ern a shake. 'If I let you go will you do that?' he said. 'Mind you, Ern, I've a good mind to put you across my knee here and now and give you the finest spanking you've ever had in your life!'

'No, Uncle!' said Ern, almost in tears. 'You let me find that fellow for you, and I'll shadow him wherever he goes. I promise you, Uncle!'

'He wears a turban,' said Mr. Larkin. 'Sort of towel round his head,' he added, as Goon looked mystified. 'Can't mistake him. He can't be far off, so let this kid go now or you'll lose the furriner.'

Goon let go Ern's arm and the boy darted off thankfully. Oh, what bad luck to run into Goon again—just as he was hoping to get some news for Fatty too! Now he had got to find and shadow someone for his uncle—someone who might have been of great use to old Fatty!

Ern remembered the lessons in shadowing that he had had from Fatty, and went silently from bush to bush, watching and listening—and soon he heard the crack of a twig on a path. Ah—the 'furriner' must be there!

Ern peeped round the bush. It was getting rather dark now but he could see a man—and he was wearing a turban!

'Nasty-looking chap,' thought Ern. 'Proper foreigner. Up to no good. Might have a knife on him somewhere so I'd better be careful!'

Ern felt very thrilled. 'Almost as if I was in a film!' he thought, remembering the dramatic moments in some of the cowboy films he had seen lately. 'Coo! What will Fatty and the others say when they hear about this!'

The man in the turban moved down the path to the little wicket-gate. Ern followed cautiously some way behind. Goon caught sight of both of them and followed cautiously too. Ern was after the man, so if he kept the boy in sight Ern would lead him to wherever the man was going!

Fatty had absolutely no idea that he was being shadowed by Ern, with Goon some distance behind. He sauntered along, thinking of Larkin, and what fun it would be to disguise himself as the old fellow, and meet with him some morning down the street! What *would* Larkin say if he came face to face with himself?

Ern followed carefully, holding his breath. Fatty went along the river-path and turned up into Peterswood village. Ern stalked him, keeping in the shadows.

Goon followed, wishing he hadn't left his bicycle behind at the Larkins. Now he would have to walk all the way back to get it that night!

Fatty suddenly felt that he was being followed, and looked round. Was he or wasn't he? Was that a figure hiding beside that bush? Well, never mind, he was nearly home!

Fatty suddenly took to his heels and ran for home, thinking that it wouldn't do to be stopped by Goon, if it *was* Goon. He had no idea it was Ern. He came to his gate and slipped through it, ran to the garden door and into the house. Up the stairs he went, two at a time, and into his bedroom. Buster welcomed him with a volley of of delighted barks.

It didn't matter what disguise Fatty put on, Buster was never deceived. Fatty always smelt like Fatty, no matter what he looked like—a 'furriner', an old man, a gypsy woman, a butcher's boy. One sniff and Buster knew him!

'Coo,' said Ern, stepping out of the shadows as Fatty went in at his gate. 'Look at that! He ran off all of a sudden, and I'm blessed if he didn't go in at Fatty's gate. Perhaps he's a friend of Fatty's. Gosh—here's Uncle!'

'Where'd that man go?' demanded Mr. Goon, holding Ern's shoulder in a vice-like grip.

'Into Fatty's gate,' said Ern. 'I say, Uncle—perhaps he's a friend of Fatty's. You'd better not go after him.'

'Ho! I'd just like to know who Master Frederick Trotteville is sending to snoop round Tally-Ho grounds,' said Goon. And in at the gate he went, leaving Ern miserably outside. Had he got Fatty into trouble?

Mr. Goon knocked loudly at the door and the maid answered promptly.

'Is Master Frederick in?' asked Goon, in his most pompous voice. Before the maid could answer Mrs. Trotteville came into the hall.

'What do you want, Mr. Goon?' she inquired. 'Was it you who knocked so loudly?'

'Er—well, yes, I suppose it was,' said Goon, forgetting to be pompous. He was rather afraid of Mrs. Trotteville. 'I came about a foreigner.'

'A foreigner?' said Mrs. Trotteville. 'But there is no foreigner here. What makes you think there is?'

'Well, he came in at your gate,' said Goon. 'Man in a turban.'

'Oh—dear me, I remember seeing a man in a turban going past the windows this afternoon,' said Mrs. Trotteville. 'I'll call Frederick. He may have seen him too.'

'Frederick!' she called up the stairs. 'Are you in?'

'Yes, Mother,' said Fatty, appearing suddenly at the top of the stairs, dressed in his ordinary clothes, and looking very clean and tidy. 'I was just reading. Do you want me?'

'Mr. Goon has come about some foreigner he thinks is here,' said Mrs. Trotteville. 'He says he came in at our gate a little while ago.'

'I think Goon must be seeing things,' said Fatty, in a concerned voice. 'Do you feel quite well, Mr. Goon? What was this fellow like?'

'He wore a turban,' said Goon, beginning to feel annoyed.

'Well, I really haven't seen anyone walking about just wearing a turban,' said Fatty. 'I think I'd have remembered if I had.'

'Don't be stupid, Frederick,' said his mother. '*I* saw somebody wearing a turban this afternoon, but as far as I could see his other clothes were ordinary ones. Who can this fellow be, Frederick?'

'A new paper-boy perhaps,' suggested Fatty. 'Or some friend of the maids? Or just somebody taking a short cut through our garden? People do, you know.'

69

'Well—this man is obviously not here, Goon,' said Mrs. Trotteville. 'I don't imagine you want to search the house?'

Goon would dearly have liked to, but Mrs. Trotteville looked so forbidding that he said a hasty good night and went off to the front gate. Fatty ushered him politely all the way and watched him stride away in the twilight.

He was just going in when a low whistle reached his ears. He swung round. Ern's voice came urgently from a bush nearby. 'Fatty! I've some news for you!'

'Ern! What in the world are you doing there?' said Fatty, startled. Out came Ern, very cautiously.

'There was a strange man snooping about in Tally-Ho grounds this afternoon,' he began. 'And I followed him to your house. He wore a turban.'

Fatty groaned. 'Fathead, Ern! That was ME! I disguised myself as a foreigner and went up and had a snoop round and a few words with our friend, Mr. Larkin! How on earth did Goon come into this?'

Ern explained sadly, feeling that he had not been at all clever. He had even taken Goon to Fatty's house! Golly, Fatty might have been caught in his disguise! What an upset that would have been. Poor Ern was really very miserable.

'Cheer up, Ern,' said Fatty, patting him on the shoulder. 'It just shows two things—one, that my disguise was really jolly good—and two, that you're certainly quick off the mark!'

Ern felt more cheerful. Good old Fatty—he always took things the right way, thought Ern. He determined to be even more on the look-out than ever. Next time he would track a *real* suspect—not just Fatty!

Fatty went up into his bedroom again, rather depressed after his interesting afternoon. This wasn't a real mystery— it was just a stupid, idiotic newspaper case!

QUITE A LOT OF TALK

FATTY WAS tremendously surprised to see the papers the next morning. Somehow they had got hold of the fact that a foreigner of some kind had been seen wandering about the grounds of Tally-Ho House.

'Mystery of the Lorenzos and Stolen Picture Flares up Again,' said one headline. 'An Old Friend found in the Grounds.'

'Indian chased by Brave Constable,' said another paper.

'Stolen Picture Probably hidden in Tally-Ho House,' said a third. 'Foreigner Found Breaking in.'

Fatty stared at these headlines in the utmost dismay. Goodness—what in the world had Goon been saying? Some reporter must have got hold of him last night and had asked if there were any news about the Lorenzos— and Goon hadn't been able to stop himself from enlarging on his encounter with the disguised Fatty.

Fatty's heart sank down into his boots. Why, Goon hadn't set even a finger on him! He had only followed Ern, who had been following him. Suppose Superintendent Jenks got to hear of this?

Fatty went round to see the others as soon as he could. They hadn't known, of course, that he was going to disguise himself as an Indian, and had been most astonished to see the papers. Larry and Daisy had gone to call for Pip and Bets, on their way down to Fatty's, and they were very pleased to see him.

'Seen the papers?' said Pip, as soon as Fatty came in at the playroom door, with Buster at his heels. Fatty nodded. The others stared at him in surprise.

'What's up? What are you looking like that for?' asked Larry. 'We were jolly pleased about it—it looks as if something might happen here after all!'

Fatty sat down and groaned in such a desperate manner that Bets ran to him at once. 'What is it? Are you ill, Fatty?'

'I *feel* ill,' said Fatty. '*I* was the Indian—didn't you guess? I thought I'd disguise myself as a foreign student, and just go for a little snoop—and of course first I bumped into old Larkin and gave him a shock—and then *Ern* discovers me and tells old Goon, who happens to be interviewing Mr. Larkin—and then Ern is told to shadow me so that Goon can see where I go.'

The others listened in horror. 'Fatty! And now you're in all the papers!'

'Yes—but mercifully nobody knows *I* was the Indian—except Ern. I told him. Wish I hadn't now. He'll never be able to keep his mouth shut. And oh—I've just thought of something else. Oh, my word!'

'What? What is it?' said Bets, quite overcome with all this. All kinds of dreadful ideas filled her mind.

'Old Larkin met me—and I asked him where my old friends the Lorenzos had gone,' said poor Fatty. 'And when he asked me for my name I told him an idiotic one —and he *wrote it down*! If Goon gets it out of him, and realizes the Indian was a spoof—in other words, me— there'll be an awful lot of fat in the fire!'

'What name did you give?' asked Larry.

'Mr. Hoho-Ha of Bong Castle, India,' said Fatty with another groan.

There was a moment's silence—and then a squeal of

laughter from Daisy. 'Oh, Fatty! Oh Mr. Hoho-Ha! Do you mean to say old Larkin *really* wrote that down?'

'Rather,' said Fatty, still unable to raise even a smile. 'It's no laughing matter, Daisy. If Ern splits on me, I'm in the soup—jolly hot soup too. We're sure to get the reporters down here then, interviewing me as the Boy who Deceived the Police! Frightful! Why did I do it?'

'Ern won't give you away,' said Bets.

'I think he *would*,' said Pip. 'He's not very brave and he's so scared of Goon that he'd say anything to get away from him.'

There came a knock at the door. Everyone turned their heads, expecting they hardly knew what. Goon perhaps—except that he wouldn't knock. He'd walk straight in!

The door opened. It was Ern! Ern, looking very flushed and rather fearful.

'Ern! We were just talking about you,' said Bets. 'Have you split on Fatty? You haven't told Goon that Fatty was the Indian, have you?'

'Coo, no,' said Ern, much to everyone's relief. 'Uncle's been at me like anything this morning—but I never said a word about Fatty. What do you take me for?'

'I knew you wouldn't, Ern,' said Bets.

'I just came to tell you something,' said Ern. 'My uncle's gone all funny-like this morning. Don't know what to make of him.'

'Exactly what do you mean?' asked Fatty, interested.

'Well—he came up to my Aunt Woosh's place this morning, though goodness knows how he found out I was staying there,' said Ern. 'And he took me into the wood-shed and shut the door. I was that scared I could hardly stand! I thought he was going to take a stick to me.'

'Poor Ern!' said Daisy.

'Well, he didn't,' said Ern. 'He was as sweet as sugar. Kept patting me on the shoulder, and telling me I wasn't such a bad kid after all—and then he said he wanted to keep me out of any unpleasantness, so he wanted me to promise I'd not say a word about how I discovered the Indian yesterday, nor a word about me shadowing him . . .'

Fatty laughed suddenly. 'Gosh! He's so proud of this Indian business that he wants everyone to think *he* discovered him, tackled him and shadowed him! He doesn't want *you* to figure in this show at all, Ern.'

'Oh—so that's it, is it?' said Ern. 'Well, my Aunt Woosh got a paper this morning, and when I saw all about you in it, Fatty—well, about the foreigner, I mean— I got the shock of my life. I was all of a tremble when my Uncle Goon came in—and I was worse when I saw him. I'm all of a tremble now, even when I think of it.'

'Have a sweet?' said Pip. 'It's good for trembles.'

Ern took one. 'Phew!' he said. 'I wasn't half glad when my uncle let me go. I promised I wouldn't say a word to anyone—and I was never so glad to promise anything in my life! Never!'

Fatty heaved a sigh of relief. 'Good old Ern,' he said, with much feeling. 'You've taken a load off my mind. If Goon goes about saying *he* discovered the Indian and tackled him, and then shadowed him, I'm all right. Though he shouldn't really say anything, if he's on a case.'

'Suppose one of the reporters from the papers finds out from Larkin that the Indian gave him the name of Mr. Hoho-Ha of Bong Castle,' said Pip. 'Won't he smell a rat?'

'No. I don't think so,' said Fatty, considering the matter. 'He'll probably think the Indian was just spoofing the old fellow. I hope Superintendent Jenks doesn't hear that, though—he'll know it's the sort of idiotic name I'd think up myself.'

'You are a one!' said Ern, round-eyed. 'How you dare! Coo, Fatty, *I* never knew it was you! You don't even *walk* like yourself when you're in disguise. You ought to be on the stage!'

'Good gracious, no!' said Fatty. 'Be on the stage when I could be a detective? Not on your life!'

'We'd better lie low for a day or two, hadn't we?' said Daisy. 'Not go anywhere near Tally-Ho House. Once this new excitement has died down, things will be all right—but Fatty oughtn't to risk anything at the moment.'

'You're right, Daisy,' said Fatty. 'But personally I'm beginning to think that the next thing we'll hear is that the Lorenzos have managed to get out of the country with the picture—and that will be that.'

'Oh, I hope not!' said Pip. 'This is a most *annoying* mystery—there's nothing to get hold of—no clues, no suspects——'

'Except the Indian,' said Larry, with a grin.

'Well—let's drop the whole thing for a couple of days,' said Fatty. 'Then we'll see if anything further has happened. We'll know by the papers.'

'Shan't I keep watch from my tree-house?' said Ern, disappointed.

'Oh yes—no harm in that,' said Fatty. 'Do those twin cousins of yours still enjoy themselves up there?'

'Oooh yes—they've got all their dolls up there now,' said Ern, sounding rather disgusted. 'There's nowhere to sit except on dolls—and one squeaks like anything if you tread on it. Gave me a real fright, I can tell you!'

They all laughed. 'Well, you let the twins sit up there as much as they like, and report to you *if* they see anything,' said Fatty. 'I wish I'd known I could be so easily seen from that tree when I wandered in yesterday. I forgot all about it! Those cousins of yours must have been keeping a pretty sharp look-out.'

'They're not bad,' said Ern. 'I've got them properly under my thumb now. They think I'm the cat's whiskers and the dog's tail and the kangaroo's jump, and . . .'

'Oh, Ern!' said Bets, and joined in the laughter. Ern beamed. He did so love the Five to laugh at any of his jokes.

'Ern, have you written any more poems?' asked Bets. Ern was very fond of writing what he called 'pomes' but as he rarely got beyond the first three or four lines, they were not very successful.

Ern pulled out a notebook, looking pleased. 'Fancy

you remembering my pomes,' he said. 'Well, I began one last week. It might be a good one—but I got stuck again.'

'What is it?' said Fatty, grinning. 'Let me help you.'

Ern read out his 'pome', putting on a very solemn voice.

> 'A pore old woman had a dog,
> And it was always barkin,
> Its name was ...'

'Well, that's as far as I've got,' said Ern. 'There's all sorts of ideas swarming round in my head, but they just sort of won't come out.'

'My dear Ern, it's a fine poem,' said Fatty earnestly. 'Don't you really know how it goes on? Listen!'

Fatty stood in the middle of the room and recited in a voice exactly like Ern's.

> 'A pore old woman had a dog,
> And it was always barkin,
> Its name was Poppet, and of course
> The woman's name was Larkin.
>
> She sniffed and coughed the whole day long,
> And said the wind was nippin,
> And when the dog got in her way
> She handed out a whippin.
>
> Her husband shuffled in and out,
> He wasn't very supple,
> They weren't at all what you might call
> A really pleasant couple!'

Fatty stopped to take breath. Ern had listened in the greatest awe. The others laughed in delight. Fatty could go on like this for ages, without stopping. It was one of the many extraordinary things he could do.

'Coo!' said Ern. 'How do you do it, Fatty? Why, that's *just* what I wanted to say in my pome but I got stuck. You're a wonder, Fatty!'

Fatty recited in a voice exactly like Ern's.

'Oh, that was just a lot of nonsense,' said Fatty, feeling much better.

'It wasn't. It was simply marvellous,' said Ern. 'I must write it all down—but it's really *your* pome now, not mine, Fatty.'

'No, it's yours,' said Fatty generously. 'I don't want it. I'd never have thought of it if you hadn't told me the first three lines. You can have it for your very own, Ern.'

Ern was delighted—and, for the next twenty minutes he didn't join in any of the fun. He was most laboriously writing out his new 'pome'.

A QUIET TWO DAYS

THERE WAS NOTHING more in the papers about the 'strange foreigner'. In fact, as far as Fatty could see, there was no mention of the Lorenzo case at all. He was rather relieved.

For two days the Five led perfectly normal lives, with Ern and Buster following them around. The Lorenzo mystery wasn't even mentioned, except that Ern volunteered the information that the twins were getting rather tired of the tree-house.

'You see, it's been windy, and their things keep falling out of the tree when the wind shakes it,' explained Ern. 'And they got annoyed because I wouldn't let them blow bubbles over the Larkins' cottage.'

'Blow bubbles over the cottage?' said Fatty, in surprise. 'But why should they want to? The bubbles would burst at once, anyhow.'

'Not the kind they've got,' said Ern. 'They aren't ordinary soap-bubbles—you make the mixture, and blow the bubbles—and they come out very big and strong—they can bump into things without breaking, so they go on flying about for ages.'

'I see,' said Fatty, having a sudden vision of Mr. and Mrs. Larkin being surrounded by big, bouncing bubbles every time they put their noses out of doors. 'Well—it does sound a most tempting thing to do, I must say—but you'd better restrain the twins at present, anyway. The tree-house spy-hole would certainly be discovered if they start anything like that.'

'I've told them not to do it,' said Ern. 'But they're not all *that* obedient, Fatty. They keep on and on about it. When they first thought of it they almost fell out of the tree with laughing.'

'Yes. Well, it's quite a bright idea,' said Fatty. 'One we might use sometime, but not just now. Come on—we are all going to the cake-shop for coffee and hot buttered scones.'

They cycled off to the cake-shop. Ern thought that this custom of the Five of popping out to eat and drink in between meals was a Very Very Good One. His aunt didn't feed him as well as his mother did, and poor Ern was in a constant state of hunger.

The cake-shop woman was very pleased to see them. Six children and a hungry dog were better than twelve grown-ups, because they seemed to eat three times as much! She brought out a plate heaped with hot, buttery scones.

'Curranty ones!' said Pip. 'Just what I like. It's decent of you to keep standing us this kind of thing, Fatty. You always seem to have a lot of money.'

'Well, this is my Christmas money,' said Fatty, who had a good supply of generous aunts and uncles and grandparents. 'Sit, Buster. Well-mannered dogs do NOT put their paws on the table, and count the number of scones.'

'They'd take some counting!' said Ern, eyeing the plate with much approval. Then he jumped violently, as a large burly figure suddenly appeared at the door.

'Oh—good morning, Mr. Goon,' said Fatty. 'Do come and join us. Do you like hot, buttery scones?'

Mr. Goon stalked in, his lips pursed up as if he was

afraid he might say something he didn't mean to. He eyed all the children, and Ern squirmed.

'I've bin looking for you,' he said to Fatty. 'Mr. Hoho-Ha! Ho yes, I've read it in Larkin's notebook. Think you've made a fool of me, don't you? Do you want me to tell the Superintendent?'

'What do you mean?' said Fatty. 'I read in the papers that you tackled a strange man very bravely the other day in the grounds of Tally-Ho House. Congratulations, Mr. Goon. I wish I'd been there.'

Ern disappeared under the table, and Buster welcomed him heartily, licking his face all over. Goon didn't even see him go.

'What do you mean—you wish you'd been there?' demanded Mr. Goon. 'You were there all right, Mr. Hoho-Ha! Just let me say this, Master Frederick Algernon Trotteville—you'd better go back to BONG CASTLE, see? Else you'll get into Very Serious Trouble.'

Having made this extraordinary fierce joke Mr. Goon marched out again. The cake-shop woman stared after him in amazement. Whatever was he talking about?

'Poor man. Mad as a hatter,' said Fatty sympathetically, reaching for another scone. 'Come out, Ern. You're safe now. Buck up, or all the scones will be gone.'

Ern came out from under the table in a hurry, still looking rather pale. He opened his mouth to ask a question.

'We're not talking about certain things just now, Ern,' said Fatty warningly, and Ern's mouth shut, only to open again for a bite at a scone.

'I suppose Goon saw all our bikes outside, and couldn't resist coming in to say a few words to you,' said Daisy in a low voice. 'I thought he was going to burst!'

The rest of the day passed very pleasantly, as Pip's mother had asked all the Find-Outers to tea and games.

'Mother says she will be out from three o'clock till seven,' said Pip. 'So if we want to make a noise or do anything silly, she says now's our chance!'

'Very thoughtful of her,' said Fatty approvingly. 'Your

81

mother is strict, Pip, but always fair. I hope your cook is in?'

Pip grinned. 'Oh yes—and she says if you go down to the kitchen and do your imitation of the gardener when she's been and picked some parsley without asking him, she'll make you your favourite gingerbread.'

'A very reasonable bargain,' said Fatty. He had once been at Pip's when the hot-tempered gardener had discovered the cook picking his parsley, 'without so much as a by-your-leaf'. Fatty had thoroughly enjoyed his remarks, and the cook had been delighted to hear Fatty acting the whole thing to the others afterwards. She had even lent him her cooking apron for an imitation gardening apron.

Fatty was amused to see the apron waiting on a chair for him. Pip chuckled. 'It must be nice to be you, Fatty,' he said. 'Getting your favourite cake because you can imitate our hot-tempered old gardener—getting the finest oranges at the greengrocer's because you do a bit of ventriloquism there, and make a cow moo at the back of the shop just to please the shop-boy—and getting . . .'

'That's enough,' said Fatty. 'You make it sound like bribery but it's merely good bargaining! Now, let's go down and do the Parsley Act straightaway, so that your cook has got plenty of time to make a smashing plate of gingerbread!'

They all went down, Ern following behind. Ern was like Bets—he thought Fatty was a wonder—there couldn't be anyone like him. He considered that he was very very lucky to be made welcome by every one of the Five. For the hundredth time he made up his mind to serve Fatty faithfully. 'Or die!' thought Ern dramatically, as he watched Fatty doing his ridiculous Parsley Act, croaking in the old gardener's voice, and flapping his apron at the enraptured cook, who was almost dying with laughter.

'Oh bless us all!' she said, wiping her eyes. 'I never saw such a thing in my life. You're old Herbert to the life. He flapped at me just like that! Stop now, I can't bear any more!'

They had their gingerbread—a magnificent pile—and old Herbert, the gardener, was immensely surprised to see Pip coming out with a very large piece for him. He took it in astonished silence.

'As a mark of gratitude from us all,' said Pip solemnly and Herbert was even more mystified.

The evening paper came just as they were all in the hall, saying good-bye to Pip and Bets. It was pushed through the letter-box and fell on to the mat. It lay there, folded in half, with the top half showing clearly. Fatty gave an exclamation as he picked it up.

'Look here! See what it says! "The Lorenzos reported in Maidenhead!" Why, that's quite near here!' He read the paragraph quickly. 'Oh well—apparently it's only just a guess by someone. Anyway, surely the Lorenzos wouldn't be foolish enough to travel about undisguised. I expect we'll keep on getting these reports from all over the country, just to keep interest alive.'

'Coo,' said Ern. 'Maidenhead! If it *was* them, they might visit Tally-Ho House—or the Larkins' cottage to get Poppet.'

'Will Goon be watching the place tonight, do you think?' asked Larry.

'I don't know. Possibly, if there *is* anything in the report,' said Fatty. 'Ern, keep your eyes skinned tonight, will you?'

'Oooh, I will,' promised Ern, thrilled. 'I wouldn't mind scouting round a bit myself—but Uncle may be about, and I wouldn't dare. I'd be sure to bump into him.'

'I'll be along before midnight,' said Fatty, making up his mind. 'Just in case.'

'Right,' said Ern, more and more thrilled. 'I'll be up in the tree-house, watching, Fatty. I'll hoot like an owl to let you know I'm there.'

He put his shut hands to his mouth, with the thumbs

83

on his lips and blew softly. Immediately the hall was filled with the sound of quavering owl-hoots.

'Jolly good,' said Larry admiringly. 'It's all right, cookie —we haven't got an owl in the hall!'

The cook, who had run out in surprise, went back into her kitchen. 'Master Frederick again, I expect,' she said to her friend sitting there. 'What a one!'

But it was Ern this time, and he hooted again, pleased to have such an admiring audience.

'Right,' said Fatty. 'You be up in the tree-house—and I'll be scouting around till midnight. I don't really expect anything to happen, but I won't leave anything to chance. I'll look out for Goon, of course.'

'Good-bye!' said Larry, hearing seven o'clock strike. 'Thank you for a lovely time. Buck up, Daisy!'

They all went off, and Pip shut the door. Ern left the others at the corner and rode back to his aunt's, full of excitement over his night's plan. The tree-house at night! He'd take a rug and some cushions, and make himself comfortable. And a bag of bull's-eyes to suck.

So, at nine o'clock, when his aunt and uncle had gone early to bed, and the twins were sound asleep in their small room, Ern sat bolt upright and listened to hear if his uncle and aunt were asleep. Yes—as usual they were both snoring—his uncle with great big, long-drawn-out snores and his aunt with little polite ones.

Ern dressed warmly, because the night was cold. He decided to take both the blanket *and* the rug off his bed. He had already put a couple of old cushions up in the tree-house, and in his coat-pocket he had the bag of bull's-eyes and a torch. Now for it!

He crept out of bed, and down the little stairway, carrying the blanket and rug. He opened the kitchen door and went out into the garden. In a minute he was at the foot of the tree. He climbed up carefully, the rugs round his neck.

He was soon in the little tree-house, peering through the peep-hole in the branches. The moon was coming up and the night was quite light. Ern popped a bull's-eye in his mouth and prepared to keep watch. He had never in his life felt so happy!

AN EXCITING TIME

FATTY did not arrive at Tally-Ho grounds till much later. His parents did not go to bed until ten past eleven that night, and Fatty waited and waited, fully dressed. He was not in disguise, because he did not intend to meet anyone if he could help it!

He had on his very thickest overcoat and a cap pulled over his thick hair. He whispered to Buster to keep quiet. The little Scottie watched him sorrowfully. He knew that Fatty meant to go out without him, and he was grieved. He wouldn't even wag his tail when Fatty gave him one last pat.

The night was light and dark alternately. When the moon sailed out from behind a big cloud the road was as bright as day. When it sailed behind a cloud, it was difficult to see without a torch. Fatty kept in the shadow of the trees, and walked softly, listening for any footsteps.

He met no one at all. Peterswood had certainly gone to bed early that night!

He went down to the river and walked along the river-path to the wicket-gate leading into Tally-Ho grounds. He felt that to go in at the front gates would certainly attract attention—and, indeed, it was possible that Goon might be there, keeping watch also. 'Though I don't really believe that Maidenhead report,' thought Fatty. 'For one thing it would be silly of the Lorenzos to try and come back so soon—and for another, if they *were* going to, they would disguise themselves too thoroughly to be easily recognized!'

He let himself in at the gate. The Larkins' cottage was in darkness, and there was not a sound. Fatty remembered that Ern would be watching from the tree-house, and he stopped under a bush to send out a hoot.

'Hoo!' called Fatty, on exactly the right note. 'Hoo-hoo-hoo-HOO!'

And back came the answer from Ern in the tree. 'Hoo! Hoo-hoo-hoo-HOO!' It was so exactly like an owl that Fatty nodded his head approvingly. Ern was good!

He began to make his way to the big house. It was in utter darkness. Fatty wished he could suddenly see a flicker or flash there, to tell him that somebody was about —that would be exciting. But everything was silence and darkness in the deserted house.

Ern hooted again. Then, before Fatty could answer, there came another hoot, and then another.

Whatever was Ern doing? Then Fatty laughed. Of course! It was real owls this time. They liked hunting on a moonlight night like this.

He thought he would send back a hoot, however, in case it *was* Ern. So he put his thumbs to his mouth and sent out a long and quavering hoot.

Immediately an answering hoot came, one that sounded quite urgent! *Was* it Ern? It was impossible to sense exactly the right direction of the hoot. Could Ern be trying to give him a message—was he warning him?

Fatty decided to stand under a thick dark bush for a while and wait quietly. The night was so silent that he might be able to pick up any noise if someone was about.

So Fatty stood absolutely still and listened. He heard nothing at all for about five minutes. Not even a hoot!

Then he was sure he heard a soft crunch as if someone was walking carefully on frosty grass. Oh, very carefully!

Fatty held his breath. Could it be one of the Lorenzos?

Had he—or she—come back to get something from the house? They would be sure to have keys. He stood still again. The moon swung out from behind a cloud and everything was suddenly lighted up. Fatty crouched back into the bush, looking round to see if he could spy anyone.

Not a sound! Not a sign of anything at all suspicious. The moon went behind a cloud again—a big cloud, this time, likely to last for some minutes.

The sound came again—a little crunch of frosted grass. Fatty stiffened. Yes—it came from round the corner of the house, he was sure of it. Someone was there—standing there—or moving very cautiously bit by bit.

A loud hoot sounded so near Fatty's head that he jumped violently. This time it really *was* an owl, for he saw the dark shadow of its wings, though he could not hear the slightest sound of the bird's flight.

The tiny crunch came again. Fatty decided that it was someone waiting there—standing on the frosty grass, and occasionally moving his feet. Who was it?

'I really must see,' thought Fatty. 'If it *is* Lorenzo I'd better scoot off and telephone Superintendent Jenks. It can't be Goon—I should hear his heavy breathing. This fellow doesn't make any sound at all, except the tiny crunching noise.'

As the moon was still behind the cloud Fatty decided he had better try and have a look at the man, whoever he was, straightaway. He made his way very very carefully from the bush, glad that the grass was not so frosty on his side of the house.

He trod unexpectedly on some dead leaves and they rustled. Fatty stopped. Had the noise been heard? He was nearly at the corner of the house now. He went forward again, and then nerved himself to peer round.

He slid his head carefully round the corner—and, very dimly, he saw a figure standing by the windows of Tally-Ho House. The figure was absolutely still. Fatty could not see any details at all, except that it seemed to be a fairly tall man. It was certainly not the short, burly Goon.

Fatty's heart began to beat fast. Who was this? He fumbled for his torch, meaning to flash it suddenly on the man's face, and then run off at top speed to telephone a warning.

He forgot about the moon! Just as he was about to switch on his torch, the moon shot out from behind the cloud, and immediately the place was flooded with light!

Fatty found himself gazing at a tall policeman in a helmet—and the policeman was also gazing at Fatty, looking most astonished! He put a whistle to his mouth and whistled shrilly, taking a step towards Fatty at the same time.

'It's all right,' began Fatty, 'I . . .'—and then, up galloped Goon from his hiding-place behind the nearby summerhouse. His mouth fell open when he saw Fatty.

Then he advanced on him in rage. 'You! You again! Don't I ever get rid of you, Toad of a Boy! You were all them owls, I suppose, hooting like mad! What you doing here? I'll tell the Chief of this. Obstructing the Course of Duty—Interfering with the Law—messing up things when we're on watch!'

'I didn't know you were watching, Goon,' said Fatty. 'I'm sorry to have disturbed you. This is honestly a mistake.'

The other policeman stood gaping in surprise. Who was this boy?

'What's your name?' he said, taking out a notebook.

'I know his name!' said Goon angrily. 'I've heard it too often, I can tell you that! This is Frederick Trotteville, and this time he's going to get into trouble. Arrest him as an Intruder on Private Property, Constable!'

'Wait a minute—is this really Frederick Trotteville?' said the other policeman. 'He's a friend of the Chief's, isn't he? I'm not arresting *him*, Goon. You can do that if you want to!'

'You do as I tell you,' said Goon, losing his temper. 'Who do you think you are, giving me my orders? You're under *my* orders tonight, P.C. Johns, as well you know.'

The moon went most conveniently behind a thick cloud at this point, and Fatty thought it would be just as well if he slipped away. He really didn't want to be arrested—and he was sorry that he had barged into Goon's little spot of night-duty. No wonder Ern had done such a lot of urgent hooting—he must have seen Goon and the other policeman wandering about in the bright moonlight!

Fatty slipped out of the wicket-gate and trotted swiftly home, pondering over what was the best thing to do. Should he ring up the Superintendent and tell him of his unfortunate meeting with Goon and his companion? Surely the Chief would know that Fatty was only trying to help?

Perhaps on the whole it would be best to leave it till the morning, and then telephone. Goon would have simmered down by then. Fatty would go and see him and apologize for barging in. Goon loved an apology!

So Fatty did not telephone, but went soberly to bed, hushing Buster's ecstatic but silent welcome. He heard an owl hooting nearby and grinned as he pulled the sheet up to his chin. Poor Goon! He must have been quite bewildered by all the owl-hoots sent out by the terrified Ern!

Ern was still up in the tree. He had an extremely good view of the grounds when the moon was out, for everything was then as distinct as in the daytime, though the shadows were very black.

Ern was shivering, not so much with cold as with excitement and panic. He had spotted Goon and his companion about eleven o'clock, before Fatty had appeared, when the moonlight had suddenly glittered on their helmets. There was no mistaking his uncle, of course—plump and stocky. The other policeman Ern didn't know.

Ern watched them walking round the big house peeping into all the windows and trying the doors. Then they disappeared. Were they expecting the Lorenzos after all? Were they hiding and lying in wait?

Old Fatty wouldn't know that! He might walk straight

into them. Ern fell into a panic and shivered so much that he shook the little tree-house from end to end.

He wondered what to do. Should he slip down the tree and go and see if he could meet Fatty and warn him? No—he didn't know which way Fatty would be coming—by the river-gate or the front gates. He might miss him!

Well, should he stay in the tree and wait for Fatty to come, and then try to warn him by hooting and hooting? But would he *see* Fatty? The moon might be in behind a cloud, and then he couldn't possibly see anyone!

Ern decided, shivering, that the best thing to do would be to wait and hope to see Fatty—and then hoot for all he was worth.

He spotted Fatty easily as the boy trod stealthily up the garden. Ern's spy-hole was indeed a good one! He hooted —and Fatty answered him. And then poor Ern spied Goon and the other policeman, standing behind the corner of the house—and now, where had Goon gone? Oh, yes, behind the summer-house! Ern hooted urgently—and to his utter disgust, an owl flew over in surprise, hooting too. Ern shook his fist at it—spoiling all his plans! Now Fatty wouldn't know one hoot from another!

Ern then saw the encounter between Fatty and Goon and the other policeman, though he could hear nothing except a murmur of voices. His eyes nearly fell out of his head with trying to see what was happening. Oh, Fatty, Fatty, make a run for it! Ern found himself saying the words over and over again.

Then the moon went behind a cloud—and when it came out again, oh joy! Ern saw a running figure on the river-path—and the two policemen hunting here and there for the vanished Fatty!

Ern heaved an enormous sigh of relief. He slumped back into the tree-house, feeling quite tired after all the suspense.

Stir yourself, Ern! The night isn't finished yet!

ERN IS MOST ASTONISHED

ERN GAVE a few more sighs, each one less enormous than the last. By now Fatty would be well on the way home. Had Goon recognized him? Ern was afraid that he had. He sat up again and peered out.

Ah—there were Goon and the other constable walking side by side, arguing. Then Goon stood and began to swing his great arms to and fro across his chest.

'He's cold,' said Ern to himself. 'Serve him right! I hope he freezes! I hope he's got to stay and watch Tally-Ho House all night long. Grrrrr!'

It was a most blood-curdling growl that Ern gave, and he even scared himself. He realized that his hands and feet were remarkably cold, and he thought longingly of his warm bed.

'I can't do anything more tonight,' he thought, beginning to climb down the tree, with the rug and blanket draped round his neck. 'I'll go back to the house.'

He climbed right down and went to the cottage. To his horror the kitchen door was now locked! He shook it quietly, filled with dismay. Who had locked it? He supposed that his uncle must have awakened at some noise—and have got up to investigate, and found the door unlocked. Blow, blow, blow!

'Well—I'm not going to knock at the door and give everybody a fright,' thought Ern. 'I'll just go back to the tree now, and explain tomorrow morning that I thought I'd like a night-out up there, and that's where I was. They'll think I'm potty, but I can't help that!'

Ern debated with himself. He would have liked another blanket. He remembered that there were piles of old newspapers in his Uncle Woosh's shed. He had heard that newspaper was a very, very warm covering, so he decided to take a few dozen papers up the tree with him.

Armed with these, he went back to the tree-house. It really seemed very cosy and comfortable after the cold air down in the yard. Ern spread out the newspaper and made himself a kind of bed. Then he wrapped a few papers round him, pulled the blanket and the rug over him, and put his head on the cushion. He had to lie curled up, because the tree-house was really very small. On the other hand Ern was not really very big!

He began to get warm. He felt quite comfortable. He yawned a huge yawn. At the same moment an owl passed by the tree and hooted.

'Hoo! Hoo-hoo-hoo-HOO!'

Ern was up like a shot. Was that old Fatty back again? He peered out of the tree but could see nothing—not even a sign of Goon and his companion. The gardens lay bathed in the brilliant moonlight, undisturbed and peaceful. The owl flew by again, and this time Ern saw it.

'Hoo!' began the owl, 'hoo, hoo . . .'

Ern put his hands to his mouth in the proper position for hooting, and joined in loudly. 'HOO-HOO-HOO-HOO!'

The owl gave a frightened 'tvit' and swerved off at once. Ern watched it go. 'Now don't you come hooting round me again!' he said. 'I've had enough of you tonight!'

And once more Ern cuddled down in his newspapers and blankets and shut his eyes! This time he fell fast asleep, and slept for about two hours.

Then a noise awakened him. At first he couldn't think where he was. He sat up in a fright. Then he saw the moonlight outside the tree and remembered. What had awakened him?

He heard a noise. It was a quiet, humming kind of noise, some way away. Was it an aeroplane? Perhaps. Was it a car far away on a road? Yes—it sounded more like that.

Ern lay down again. He shut his eyes. Then he heard another noise and sat up.

Splash! Splash-splash! Ern looked out of the tree again. Was somebody swimming in the river at this time of night? No—not on a frosty night in January! Still—there was that soft splash-splash again! Ern strained his eyes over towards the river.

He saw something white sailing on it—two white things —and one or two shadowy ones behind. He laughed.

'It's the swans—and their babies! I'm daft! Imagining all kinds of things when it's only a couple of swans and their family. Well, fancy them keeping awake all night! I thought they put their heads under their wings and slept.'

Ern lay down again, determined that he wouldn't be disturbed by any more noises. There was no sign of Goon now, or of his companion. The owl had stopped hooting. The swans had stopped splashing. He didn't mean to let himself be disturbed by ANYTHING else!

He was soon half-asleep. Small noises came to him on the night-wind, and once he thought he heard voices, but was sure he was dreaming. He imagined he heard a dog barking and half-opened his eyes. Yes, it was. Probably Poppet—it sounded exactly like her high little bark. She'd get slapped for waking the couple up in the middle of the night!

Ern fell into such a sound sleep that not even the owl awoke him when it came and sat on his very tree, and gave a sudden mournful hoot. Ern slept on. Dawn came slowly, and the sun sent golden fingers into the sky. Soon it would be light.

Ern awoke. He sat up, bewildered, but then remembered everything. He'd better get up and climb down the tree. His aunt would wonder where he was—she must be up and about.

Ern was just about to climb down the tree when he

heard shouting. Loud, angry shouts—and then he heard bangs—bang-bang-bang! BANG, BANG, BANG! Gracious goodness, what was all that? Ern slithered down the tree and went to the hedge and listened. The noise came from somewhere in the grounds of Tally-Ho House. Ern wondered what it was. It couldn't be Fatty back again, and in trouble, surely!

He slipped through the hedge and went by the Larkins' cottage. The door opened and the old man came out, plump in his old overcoat, his scarf and cap on as usual. He limped over to Ern.

'What's that noise?' he said, in his hoarse voice. 'You go and see. My wife's ill today and I don't want to leave her.'

Ern nodded at the dirty old man and went cautiously in the direction of the noise. It grew louder. BANG-BANG! HELP! LET US OUT! BANG-BANG!

Ern was mystified. Who was locked in and where—and why? It wasn't Fatty's voice, thank goodness.

Ern went in the direction of the noise. It sounded round the further corner of the house, where the boiler-house was. Ern turned the corner and saw the small boiler-house not far off.

Yes—the noise was coming from there. Ern looked at the little place fearfully. He wasn't letting anyone out till he knew who they were!

He went cautiously up to the boiler-house and stood on a box outside to look in at the small window. He was so astounded at what he saw that he fell off the box.

Inside the boiler-house, furiously angry, were Mr. Goon and the other policeman! Their helmets were hanging on a nail. Ern saw two hot, furious faces upturned to him as he appeared at the window, and heard more loud shouts.

'Open the door! ERN! What you doing here? OPEN THE DOOR AND LET US OUT!'

Goon had been most astonished to see Ern's scared face at the tiny little window, but very thankful. Now perhaps they could get out of this stifling boiler-house and get something to eat and drink.

'Why did we ever come in here?' groaned Goon, as he heard Ern struggling with the large, stiff key in the outer side of the door. 'It was so cold, and it seemed such a good idea to light up the boiler and shut the door and have a little warm!'

'Must have been the fumes that sent us off to sleep so sudden-like,' said his companion dolefully. 'I feel as if my head's bursting. Drat that boy—why can't he unlock the door?'

'Buck up, Ern, you dolt!' roared Mr. Goon. 'We're cooking-hot in here.'

'Who locked us in?' said the other man. 'That's what *I* want to know. It wouldn't be the Lorenzos, would it now? They couldn't have come after all, could they?'

'No! I've told you—it was that boy Frederick Trotteville—the one we found here last night,' said Goon crossly. 'One of his funny tricks—ho, he'll laugh on the other side of his face this time. I go straight to the Chief about this—dead straight! Locking us into a boiler-house—why we might have been dead with the fumes this morning! ERN—what you doing out there? You've only got to turn the key. Are you asleep, boy?'

'No, Uncle. And don't you talk to me like that when I'm doing my best to help you,' panted Ern. 'It's a whopping big key and very rusty. I've a good mind to leave you here if you don't talk proper to me when I'm trying hard.'

Mr. Goon was amazed to hear this cheek from Ern. But he had to swallow his wrath and speak in honey-like tones, afraid that Ern really would go off and leave them.

'Now, Ern—it's only because we're almost cooked,' he said. 'I know you're doing your best. Ah—there's a good lad—the key's turned!'

Ern fled as his uncle and the second policeman walked out of the boiler-house. One look at their beetroot-like faces and protruding eyes was enough for him. Goon and his companion walked with as much dignity as they could muster past the Larkins' cottage on their way to the river.

The old fellow came out of his door, shuffling as usual. 'What was the matter?' he said, in his hoarse voice.

'Tell you later,' said Goon, who was not particularly anxious that the tale of the boiler-house should go all round Peterswood. 'Nothing much. We just kept watch last night, that's all. You didn't hear anything, did you? We never heard a sound—so we're going off-duty now.'

Mr. Goon went back to his house and took up the telephone, a grim look on his face. He made a brief report, which caused quite a stir at the other end. It even made the Chief himself come to the telephone.

'Goon? What's this story about Frederick Trotteville? I don't believe it.'

'Sir, I wouldn't tell you such a story if it wasn't true,' said Goon earnestly. 'And P.C. Johns, who was with me, will tell you that this boy was in the grounds last night, snooping round after us—one of his little jokes, sir, this was. He thought it would be funny to lock us in.'

'But what were you doing in the boiler-house, Goon, when you should have been outside on duty?' said the Chief's sharp voice.

'Just looking round, sir,' said Goon, and then let his imagination get the better of him. 'We heard footsteps outside, sir, then the door banged and the key turned in the lock, and we heard Master Frederick's laugh, sir—a most horrible laugh, sir, and . . .'

'That's enough, Goon,' said the Chief's voice. 'All right. I'll see to this. Did you hear or see anything at all last night?'

'Nothing at all, sir,' said Goon, and then the telephone was clicked off at the Chief's end. Goon stood quite still, his face red with delight.

'Ho, you Toad of a Boy,' he said. 'Now you've gone too far at last. You're finished!'

FATTY IS PLEASED

FATTY was just going down to breakfast when a big black police car swept up the drive to the front door, and out got Superintendent Jenks, looking rather grim. Fatty was thrilled.

'He's got some news! And he wants me to help in some way!' thought Fatty joyfully. He went to open the door himself.

'I want a word with you, Frederick,' said the Chief, and Fatty led him into the study, struck with the Superintendent's sharp voice.

Once the door was shut, the Chief looked straight at Fatty.

'What possessed you to lock Goon and the other fellow up last night?' he demanded grimly.

Fatty stared in surprise. 'I don't know what you mean, sir,' he said at last. 'I really don't. Where am I supposed to have locked them up? In the cells?'

'Don't play the fool,' said the Chief, his eyes like gimlets, boring into poor Fatty. 'Don't you realize that you can go a bit too far with your jokes on Goon?'

'Sir,' said Fatty earnestly, 'do believe me when I say I haven't the remotest idea what you are talking about. I saw Goon last night, in the grounds of Tally-Ho House, where I was keeping watch in case the Lorenzos turned up—I had seen a report that they had been spotted at Maidenhead. Goon had another policeman with him. I left

98

the grounds a few minutes after I had seen them and said a few words to them, and went straight home to bed. They were not locked up when I left them. I must ask you to believe me, sir. I never tell lies.'

The Chief relaxed, and sat down. 'Right, I believe you, of course, Frederick,' he said. 'But I must say it's queer how you always turn up in the middle of things. Goon and Johns were locked up all night in the boiler-house at Tally-Ho, and Ern let them out this morning.'

'Ern!' said Fatty, startled.

'Yes, *he* seemed to be about too,' said the Chief. 'Goon and Johns were apparently half-cooked, the boiler-house was so hot.'

'The boiler wasn't going when I left them, sir,' said Fatty. 'I'd have noticed if it was—I'd have seen the glow when I went near it.'

'Oh. Then who lit it?' said the Chief.

'Goon and Johns, I suppose,' said Fatty. 'It was a cold night, and they might have thought it a good idea to light up the boiler and have a warm, sir. And possibly they—er —well, quite possibly they fell asleep.'

'Yes. That thought also occurred to me,' said the Chief.

'It might have been the fumes that sent them off, of course,' said Fatty generously. 'They might not have meant to sleep there—only get warm.'

'Yes. Quite so,' said the Superintendent: 'Still, the fact remains that SOMEBODY locked them in.'

'Yes. WHO?' said Fatty. 'Do you think the Lorenzos *could* have slipped back, sir—for some reason or other— perhaps to fetch the little poodle Mrs. Lorenzo is so fond of—or even to get something from the house?'

'It's possible,' said the Chief. 'Yes, quite possible. They've a reputation for being dare-devils. We'll find out if the dog is gone—or if the house has been entered and anything personal taken—something that they had left behind and wanted. What a fathead that fellow Goon is, isn't he? Still, I'm glad I came over here. I'd like you to take a hand now, in this mystery, Frederick.'

'Oh—thank you very much, sir,' said Fatty, thrilled.

'I'm not telling Goon this, because he's such a blunderer,' said the Chief, 'but I have a distinct feeling that the Lorenzos are back in Peterswood for some reason or other —perhaps as you say, to get back the dog. Mrs. Lorenzo is quite mad about it—idolizes it—and I think it possible that they will try to get it. Or again, it's just possible that they didn't take the picture with them, but have left it behind in case they were caught—for some accomplice to fetch.'

'But what about the crate they were said to have been seen with up north?' asked Fatty.

'That might have been a blind to put us off,' said the Chief. 'They're clever, these Lorenzos. You wouldn't believe the things they've done—and got away with, too. They are about the cleverest tricksters I've had to deal with.'

'Well, I'll be proud to help,' said Fatty, as the Chief got up to go. 'Is there any particular thing you'd like me to do?'

'No. Go your own way. Do what you like,' said the Chief. 'Short of locking Goon up in a boiler-house, of course! Though I feel very like doing that myself this morning!'

Fatty saw him off and went into the breakfast room feeling most elated. So Goon had told the Chief a thumping big lie about him, had he? Well, it hadn't done him any good. He, Fatty, was now more or less in charge of something that was turning out to be jolly interesting—in fact, a very promising mystery!

Ern came to see Fatty immediately after his breakfast. He had had to do a lot of explaining to his aunt about his night in the tree-house, but it was over at last. Now all he wanted to do was to tell Fatty about Goon and his companion in the boiler-house—and how they had said that it was Fatty who locked them in.

'*Did* you, Fatty?' said Ern, looking at him in awe. He was half-disappointed when Fatty shook his head.

'No, Ern. Much as I wish I could have done it, I didn't. Ern, you were up in that tree all night you say. Did you hear or see anything at all?'

'Well, owls, of course,' said Ern. 'What with you and me and the owls *all* hooting . . .'

'I don't mean owls,' said Fatty. 'Think hard, Ern—did you hear any out-of-the-way sounds at all?'

Ern thought back to his night in the tree. 'Well, I heard a kind of humming noise,' he said. 'I thought at first it was an aeroplane. But it might have been a car.'

'Ah,' said Fatty. 'Go on. Anything else?'

'I heard splashing, and saw the swans swimming in the moonlight,' said Ern. 'They looked as white as snow. And I *thought* I heard voices once, and a dog barking.'

Fatty was alert at once. 'Voices? A dog barking? Would that be Poppet?'

'Yes. I think it was,' said Ern. 'Her bark is sort of high, isn't it?—more like a yelp.'

'You're *sure* about the voices?' said Fatty. 'And the barking? You see, *some*body besides me and Goon and Johns must have been there last night—and locked them up!'

'Coo yes,' said Ern. 'Lot of people about last night, it seems! Well, these voices and barking were some time after you'd left. I tell you, I was half-asleep by then.'

'You couldn't have heard voices unless they had been fairly *near*,' said Fatty, frowning and thinking hard. 'Would they have been in or near the Larkins' cottage, do you think?'

'Well—I don't reckon I'd have heard them if they'd been *inside* the cottage,' said Ern. 'I'd have heard them *outside* all right.'

'Did Poppet's bark sound pleased or frightened?' asked Fatty.

'Pleased,' said Ern, at once.

'Oh. That's interesting,' said Fatty. '*Very* interesting. Ern, I think the Lorenzos came to get their dog from the Larkins last night—and perhaps to get a few things from the big house as well. They saw Goon and Johns asleep as they passed the boiler-house and neatly locked them in.'

'You're right, Fatty,' said Ern, in great admiration. 'It's wonderful to see how you work these things out. Well, if the dog's gone, we'll *know* it was the Lorenzos who were there last night.'

'Yes. But it doesn't *really* get us any further forward,' said Fatty. 'I mean—we still shan't know where the Lorenzos are—or where the picture is either.'

'You'll find all that out too, Fatty, straight you will,' said Ern solemnly. 'You and your brains!'

'You go and tell the others to meet down in my shed at half-past nine,' said Fatty. 'We'll all have a talk together.'

So, at half-past nine, the whole company was gathered together in the little shed, and heard the grand tale of the night in the grounds of Tally-Ho, and all that had happened there. Pip was so tickled to hear about Goon and Johns being locked in the boiler-house that he laughed till he ached.

'Now the first thing we must do is to go up to the Larkins and find out about Poppet,' said Fatty. 'If she's gone, it proves that the Lorenzos were there last night. We'll then put the Larkins through a lot of questions, and try to get out of them what really did happen last night.'

'Right,' said Larry. 'Let's go now.'

'We shan't be able to see *Mrs.* Larkin,' said Ern. 'She's ill. I saw old Bob Larkin this morning when I went to set Mr. Goon free. He heard the shouting and banging too.'

'Well—we can perhaps get something out of Larkin,' said Fatty. 'Everyone got their bikes?'

Everyone had. Buster was put into Fatty's basket, and off they all went. They chose the river-path again because the Larkins' cottage was so near it.

They leaned their bikes against the railings, and marched up the path to the cottage. Fatty knocked on the door.

It opened—and out came Mr. Larkin, still with his cap and scarf on, though he had discarded his overcoat and now wore a shapeless, baggy old tweed jacket.

'Oh—what do you want?' he said in his hoarse voice, peering through the thick lenses of his glasses at the six silent children. When he saw Buster he shut the door behind him, and stood just outside it.

'Er—Mr. Larkin—could we have a word with you?' asked Fatty.

'I don't charge nuffin' for that,' said the man. 'What's up?'

'Er—could we come inside? It's a bit cold out here,' said Fatty, feeling certain that Mr. Larkin had carefully shut the door behind him so that they couldn't see that the little dog was no longer running about inside.

'You can come in if you leave your dog outside,' said the man. 'I don't want the little poodle upset. She's over-excited today.'

Fatty stared. It sounded as if the poodle was still there! 'She's in her basket, beside my wife,' said Larkin hoarsely. He coughed.

'Oho!' thought Fatty, 'so *that's* going to be the tale! His wife's not well—keeps to her bed—and the poodle keeps her company—though really it has been taken away in the night. Very clever. The Lorenzos must have thought that out!'

'I'd like to see the poodle,' said Bets suddenly, seeing that Fatty was now in a difficulty. 'Can I go into your wife's room and stroke her?'

'No,' said the man. The children looked at one another. Very, very suspicious!

And then something surprising happened. A loud ex-cited barking came from the little cottage—then a patter of feet could be heard—and then the little white poodle appeared at the kitchen window, her nose pressed against the pane as if she was looking for Buster! *How* all the children stared!

A RECAP!

ALL THE SIX stared at Poppet as if they couldn't believe their eyes! As for Buster, he nearly went mad with excitement to see the dear little poodle with her nose at the window, looking down at him.

Poppet wagged her tail hard and barked loudly. She seemed full of life and happiness—quite different from when they had seen her before.

'I suppose she's so pleased because she saw her beloved mistress last night—but did she, after all? We just thought it must be the *Lorenzos* who had come and gone—and fetched Poppet. But it might have been anyone, now, because Poppet is still here! Gosh—I've got to work things out all over again!' Fatty frowned as he stood looking at the dog.

Mr. Larkin stood blinking at the children through his thick glasses. He wiped his sleeve across his nose and began to shuffle away, half limping as he went.

'Mr. Larkin!' called Fatty. 'Just half a minute—did you hear much disturbance last night? Did you see anyone—or do you know who locked up the two policemen?'

Larkin shook his head. 'I heerd noises,' he said. 'But I didn't stir from out my bed.'

He shuffled off towards the boiler-house, and the children watched him go.

Fatty peered into the window

Fatty looked back at the little cottage. Somebody *had* come there last night—Ern had heard voices and that meant that people were talking outside the cottage. Larkin was not telling the truth when he said he had not stirred from his bed. He *had* left his bed to open his door and talk to someone. Had he taken a message? Had he—ah yes—had he perhaps taken in a parcel—a *crate*? It would surely be an ingenious idea to bring the picture back and store it in the little cottage!

He went to the window where Poppet was still barking, pawing at the pane excitedly. He looked in cautiously, trying to see what was in the small room. It was a poor, dirty place, with makeshift furniture. There was certainly no crate there, or large, wrapped-up parcel.

There was no sign of Mrs. Larkin. Larkin had told Ern she was ill, so presumably she was in bed in the back room.

A thought suddenly struck him. Could the Larkins *possibly* be hiding the Lorenzos? The couple were apparently unable to get out of the country, and must be on the run, hiding here and there—running the risk of being spotted. It would be a clever thing to do to come and hide in the very place where no one would think they would dare to be!

There didn't seem anything else to do now but walk away. Now that Poppet *was* still there, after all, new plans would have to be made, and new ideas thought of. Especially some plan that would bring in the possibility of searching the cottage in case the Lorenzos *were* hiding there!

'Larry! Pip! Let's go!' called Fatty. 'Hey, Buster, stop trying to paw down the wall under Poppet's window. Come on, Bets and Daisy—you coming too, Ern? Let's go back to my shed and talk.'

They left Poppet still barking happily at the window, her stiff tail wagging hard. There was no sign of Larkin. He was presumably raking out the boiler-fire, still warm from the night before.

They all rode off together, Fatty thinking hard. They piled their bicycles against Fatty's shed, and went in. Fatty lighted the little oil-stove.

'Biscuits on that shelf, Larry,' he said. 'Lemonade below—or shall we have cocoa? I feel cold.'

Everyone voted for cocoa, and Pip was sent up to the kitchen to ask for milk.

'We can boil it on the oil-stove as usual,' said Fatty. 'Daisy, will you see to it?'

It was soon cosy and warm in the shed, and the milk boiled quickly on the top of the stove. Everyone sat down on boxes or rugs, Ern too. He loved times like this. He gazed round the shed in awe—coo, the things that old Fatty had there!

Fatty's shed was indeed a medley of all kinds of things —old clothes of every kind for disguises—a few wigs hanging on nails—boxes of make-up, with many kinds of moustaches inside, as well as grease-paint and powder. There was on end to the fascinating array. There was even a postman's hat and uniform! Now how in the world did Fatty get that, Ern wondered.

Once they were all supplied with biscuits and hot cocoa, Fatty began to talk.

'I think the time has come for a recap,' he said. 'We . . .'

'What's a recap?' said Bets, much to Ern's relief. He too had no idea what Fatty meant by a 'recap' but did not dare to ask.

'Oh—recap is short for recapitulation,' said Fatty. 'I . . .'

'Yes, but I don't know what recapit—pit—whatever you said is either,' said Bets.

'Dunce!' said Pip, in his brotherly way.

'All right—you tell her what it is, Pip,' said Fatty, at once.

'Well, it's—it's—well, I don't exactly know how to explain it, but I know what it means,' said Pip.

'Dunce!' said Fatty, and turned to Bets. 'A recap just means I'll go quickly over all that has happened, so as to give us a clear picture—and then it makes future planning easier. Got it, Bets?'

'Oh yes,' said Bets gratefully. 'Go ahead, Fatty.'

Fatty began. 'Well, the tale begins when we all saw the Lorenzos that day at the station, being seen off by their friends. Poppet was with them—but was given to old Larkin who had apparently been told to fetch her and take her home when the Lorenzos had departed in the train. He ____ with her under his coat. Correct?'

'____,' said everyone.

'____ he next thing we heard was that the police were aft___ Lorenzos because they had apparently been clever enough to steal a very valuable picture from some picture gallery. They probably meant to leave this country with it and sell it abroad somewhere. Correct?'

'Correct,' chorused everyone.

'They were then spotted here and there, and apparently gave up the idea of trying to get out of the country for the time being. A crate was seen in a car which they stole to get away from one of their hiding-places—presumably containing the picture.'

'But, Fatty, they only had two little suitcases with them when we saw them,' said Daisy. 'No crate at all.'

'Well, they wouldn't go off on a journey with an enormous crate!' said Fatty. 'I imagine that after they had stolen the picture, frame and all, they got some friend of theirs, someone as dishonest as themselves, to hide the picture for them—and have it crated and put ready for them at some place where they could call for it.'

'So wherever they go they've got to take the picture with them now, I suppose?' said Pip. 'A bit of a nuisance, I should think!'

'A *great* nuisance!' said Fatty. 'But unless they can undo the crate, destroy it, take out the picture and hide it somewhere really safe, they've *got* to carry it around!'

'And that's what they've been doing,' said Larry. 'And I bet they've brought it here and hidden it somewhere! I bet they came last night with it!'

108

'I was coming to that,' said Fatty. 'It does seem to me that if they *were* seen at Maidenhead they would not have come so near their home if they were not making for it for some reason. And the only reasons that are possible are—to hide the picture, and to take Poppet.'

'And they *didn't* take Poppet,' said Bets.

'No they didn't, so we were wrong there,' said Fatty. 'Well, I think perhaps we were silly to think they'd take that little poodle. Once it had disappeared from the Larkins, the police would have been told to keep a watch-out for a couple with a beautiful little poodle—you can't hide a dog if it's with you all the time!'

'They could have dyed it black,' said Bets.

'Oh yes—they would certainly have done that,' said Fatty. 'But it would still be a poodle—and would arouse suspicion, black, white or red, if the police were looking for one accompanying a couple of people in a hotel, or boarding-house or wherever the Lorenzos went.'

'I suppose we come now to last night,' said Pip. 'Ern's the only one who really knows about that.'

'Yes. Ern, relate what you know,' said Fatty. 'We already know it, but it might clear things a bit, and make us think of something new.'

Ern cleared his throat and stood up as if he were going to recite in class.

'Well—I was asleep in the tree-house and a noise woke me up—sort of humming noise, like an aeroplane or car. Then after a bit I heard splashing and I looked out and saw the swans on the river, sailing on the water. Fine they looked, too. Then I went to sleep—and I woke up again thinking I heard voices not far off—maybe outside the Larkins' cottage—and I heard Poppet barking madly— sort of happy-like. That's all.'

Ern sat down abruptly, blushing red. Everyone felt as if they really ought to clap, but nobody did. Bets gave him an admiring smile and Ern felt proud of himself.

'Now we come to this morning, when we all go off expectantly to the Larkins' cottage, feeling sure that Poppet will be gone—and lo and behold, she is there, as happy as a sand-boy!' said Fatty.

'Which is a bit funny,' said Larry, 'because the Larkins haven't been nice to her, as *we* know!'

'Yes,' said Fatty. 'Well—there's our recap, Bets. Now—has anyone any remarks to make or any good suggestions.'

'I'm sure the Lorenzos were there last night, because Poppet is so happy this morning,' said Pip.

'I thought that too,' said Bets. 'But now I'm wondering! If they had come *and gone* last night wouldn't Poppet be down in the dumps again?'

'You've got a point there, Bets,' said Fatty.

'I say! Perhaps they're still there!' said Pip. 'Hiding in the cottage!'

'Yes. Or perhaps in the house,' said Daisy, 'the *big* house, I mean. They would have keys, wouldn't they?'

'Oh yes,' said Fatty. 'Actually it did cross my mind that the Larkins might be hiding the Lorenzos. It would make the cottage very crowded though—and the Larkins would be scared in case the police came to search. But Poppet is so very happy that I can't help thinking they are still somewhere about. *Mrs.* Lorenzo anyhow!'

'Fatty! Can't we somehow manage to look in the cottage?' said Bets. 'Oh, do think of some way. It would be too marvellous if *we* discovered the Lorenzos, after the police have been looking for them for ages!'

'Right. That's a good plan,' said Fatty. 'Does anyone happen to know if the cottage has got electric light? I didn't notice. Very remiss of me!'

'Yes. It has,' said Larry, surprised. 'Fatty! What are you going to do? I *know* you've got a plan. What is it?'

OFF TO TALLY-HO HOUSE

FATTY certainly had a plan. That was quite clear. His eyes shone and he looked excited.

'Yes! I'll tell you what I'll do! I'll dress up as an electricity man, and go to the Larkins' cottage to read the meter!' He looked round at the others with a broad grin.

Larry slapped him on the back. 'Wizard! You can get right in then and it wouldn't take you a minute to see if there was any place for people to hide in that tiny cottage. There can only be three rooms at the most—all downstairs. There's no second storey.'

'It's a pity Mrs. Larkin is ill, or you could have gone today,' said Bets.

'Blow!' said Fatty. 'I forgot that for the moment. I can't very well go blundering into the cottage if she's sick in bed.'

'I'll watch from the tree-house,' said Ern, excited. 'If I see her about I'll nip along and tell you, Fatty. I'll sit up there all the afternoon.'

'Right,' said Fatty. 'Well—anyone else got any suggestions or brain-waves?'

'I was wondering how the Lorenzos arrived last night,' said Daisy. 'If they came by car—which would be rather a silly thing to do, I should think—wouldn't the car be hidden somewhere in the grounds? That's if the Lorenzos themselves are still in hiding there, I mean. Unless, of course, someone drove them there and dropped them. It might have been the car that Ern heard.'

'That's a point, too,' said Fatty. 'We could go up to the grounds this afternoon, and have a look at the drive entrances. If we see recent tracks we'll know a car came last night—and we'll look for it!'

'Another thing,' said Pip, 'can we find out if the big house has been entered by the Lorenzos? They might even have been daring enough to go into it and hide the picture there. The house has been already searched for that—so it might be a jolly good hiding-place.'

'Yes. We can find that out too,' said Fatty. 'I could ring up the Superintendent to ask him if he's had any report about it.'

'Well—we're getting on!' said Pip. 'My mind is certainly a lot clearer since our recap!'

'I don't see that there's anything more we can suggest,' said Larry. 'At the moment we are going on the hope that the Lorenzos came by car last night, hid it in the grounds, got into the big house, hid the picture there, went to the Larkins and woke them up, and persuaded them to let them into the cottage to hide till all the hoo-ha has blown over.'

'Right!' said Fatty. 'You put that very well, Larry. This has been a very good conference—*real* detectives couldn't have had a better one! Now let me see—my first job is to ring up the Superintendent and ask if he knows whether the house was entered last night or not. Next, we must go up this afternoon and examine the drive entrances. Third, I must disguise myself as a meter-reader, and see if I can examine the cottage.'

'Meter-readers carry a kind of card backed by a board with elastic round, don't they?' said Daisy. 'I know ours does. And a peaked cap—and a torch to read the meter. That's all. Ours doesn't have a uniform.'

'I'll find out from our cook,' said Fatty. 'But I don't think it much matters what I wear really, so long as I produce a card and flourish a torch, and announce "Come to read your meter, Mam!" in a loud voice.'

They all laughed. "You'll get into the cottage all right if you say it like that!' said Bets.

'I say! What about you dressing up in whatever you're going to wear, and coming with us to examine the drive entrances,' said Larry. 'You can put your torch and cap and card into your pocket to use if we find out that Mrs. Larkin is out and about again. Otherwise you'd be sitting at home waiting for Ern to nip down and fetch you as soon as he saw any sign of Mrs. Larkin. And if he *doesn't* see anything of her, you'll be moping at home all alone!'

'Yes. That's an idea,' said Fatty. 'Ern, listen—you can do what you suggested this afternoon, and sit up in the tree-house, with a whistle—and if you see anything of Mrs. Larkin, just whistle three times, because we shall be somewhere snooping around the grounds.'

'Whistle *twice* if you want to warn us about anything—Goon or strangers and so on,' said Larry. 'Three times for Mrs. Larkin.'

'And I'll then come up to the cottage and do my meter-reading act,' said Fatty. 'Well—is that all understood?'

'Yes,' said everybody.

'Be here at two-thirty,' said Fatty. 'We'll all go together —except you, of course, Ern. You'll be up in the tree as soon after your dinner as you can, won't you?'

'Yes, Fatty,' said Ern importantly. Then he leapt to his feet with a yell that startled everyone considerably and set Buster barking madly.

'Coo—look at the time! Twenty to one and my Aunt Woosh said I was to be back by half-past twelve. I won't get no dinner at all! So-long, everybody!'

Ern disappeared up the garden path at top speed, Buster running excitedly beside him. Everyone laughed. Good old Ern!

That afternoon at half-past two everyone but Ern was outside Fatty's house with their bicycles. Fatty, looking rather peculiar, came out with his, Buster with him.

'Are you going to take Buster?' said Bets, pleased. 'I didn't think you would.'

'Well, I can leave him with you if Ern gives the signal for me to go and do some meter-reading!' said Fatty. 'He does so badly want to come—don't you, Buster?'

'Wuff!' said Buster joyfully. He couldn't bear it when the children went off without him. He ran beside the bicycles as they all rode off. Fatty said the run would take off some of his fat, and it wasn't too far for him to run all the way to the river.

'Wait—we're not *going* to the river-path this time!' said Larry, as they all turned down the river-road. 'We've forgotten—we're going to the drive-gates that open on to the lane that leads out of the main road.'

'So we are!' said Pip, and they all swerved the other way. Bets looked at Fatty and giggled.

'You don't really look respectable enough to come riding with us,' she said. 'Did you *have* to make yourself so untidy, Fatty?'

'Not really,' said Fatty, with one of his grins. 'I just let myself go, rather!'

He wore an old suit, too big for him, no collar but a scarf instead, and had brushed his hair over his forehead instead of back. In his pocket was a cap with a black shiny peak, a card with figures scribbled on it, backed by a small board, a pencil tied to it with string, and a torch.

'No Electricity Board would employ *you* as a meter-reader,' said Bets. 'For one thing, you're not only untidy but you don't look *old* enough.'

'Oh, I'll soon remedy *that*!' said Fatty, and put his hand into his pocket. He pulled out a silly little moustache and stuck it on his upper lip. At once he looked older. Bets laughed.

'You look really *dreadful*! I'm sure no one would ever let you into their house!'

They turned off the main road and came into the little lane that led to the entrance gates of Tally-Ho. They got off when they came to the big gate-posts.

The big double gates were shut. There were two at each entrance to the long, curving drive. Fatty looked at them.

'Well! Whoever drove in there with a car would have quite a business opening those big gates—they're so heavy. I wonder why they're shut.'

'So that people can't drive in, I suppose,' said Larry. 'Fatty, did you ring up the Chief about the house—to know if by any chance anyone had got into it last night?'

'Yes, I did. And apparently even if the Lorenzos had keys to the back, front and side-doors it wouldn't be any good,' said Fatty. 'All the doors have been bolted inside, except a side-door. The police bolted them all—and got out by the side-door, in which they have had a special lock fitted. So nobody can get in except the police—and they only by the side-door! Apparently there are a lot of valuable things in Tally-Ho belonging to its real owner—the one who let the house furnished to the Lorenzos.'

'Oh. Well then we needn't bother about the house,' said Larry. 'We'll just concentrate on trying to find out if a car came here last night, and is hidden away somewhere.'

Fatty was looking at the ground, which was very frosty that day. 'There are wheel-marks,' he said, 'but I can't tell if they are old or new. Anyway, of course, they might be the marks of any police-car that has been here.'

Pip had gone up to the gates to look through them. He gave a sudden exclamation. 'Look here—no car could come through these gates—they have a wooden bar nailed across them!'

The others went to see. Pip was right. A bar was nailed right across each of the double gates. Obviously the police did not mean anyone to go to the house at the moment!

'Well, that rather rules out the Lorenzos coming by car, and leaving it in the grounds,' said Fatty. 'Let's go to the river-path entrance, and see if Mr. Larkin is any-where about. He might have something to say for once. You never know!'

They went back, and took the road down to the river-path. They were soon standing outside the wicket-gate.

'Look!' said Bets. 'The swans again. What a pity we haven't any bread for them!'

They stood and watched them, the big swans leading the little cygnets to the bank. A boat came by, the oars splashing in the water with a pleasant noise. The swans swam off out of the boat's way.

'Splash-splash!' said Bets, remembering something. 'Ern said he remembered hearing splashes in the night. I wonder now—could he have heard a *boat*?'

'Gosh! I never thought of that!' said Fatty. 'A boat! Yes, they could have come by boat, of course! Let's look and see if there's one in the boat-house—that's the boat-house belonging to Tally-Ho over there, isn't it?'

It was. It was not locked. The children pushed the little door open and looked inside. A small boat lay there, bobbing gently on the little ripples that ran into the boat-house.

Fatty looked at it. Its name was Tally-Ho, so there was no doubt that it belonged there. He was about to step into it when he stopped. A shrill sound had come to his ears.

'Ern's whistle!' he said. 'My goodness, he must have got hold of a *police*-whistle! What a row! He's whistled three times—that is to say he's seen Mrs. Larkin. I'll go and do my meter-reading. Have a look round the boat-house while I'm gone, you others. I'll join you later!'

SOME VERY GOOD IDEAS

FATTY pulled on his cap with the black peak, and smoothed his ridiculous little moustache. He tightened the scarf round his neck, and off he went. The others grinned at one another.

'He'll be reading that meter in two minutes!' said Pip. 'I wish I was with him to see what happens.'

Fatty strode off to the wicket-gate and went through it, whistling loudly. He marched straight up to the door—and then saw Mrs. Larkin outside, with Poppet dancing about.

She looked round at him, startled. She really was a peculiar-looking person with her extraordinary wig, her dead-white face, and dark glasses. She sniffed loudly.

'What is it?' she said hoarsely, and coughed. She took out a dirty handkerchief from behind her dull red shawl, and wiped her nose vigorously. She coughed again and kept her handkerchief over her mouth, as if the cold air was too much for her.

'You've got a bad cold, Mam,' said Fatty politely. 'Sorry to bother you, but I've come to read the meter, if it's convenient.'

The woman nodded. She went to the little clothes-line and began to take down some washing. Fatty took his chance and went into the house at once, hoping that Mr. Larkin was not there.

There was no one in the front room. Fatty took a hurried look round, and could see nowhere at all for anyone to hide. He went into a back room—a small bedroom in which the bed took up most of the room. Nobody was there either. Fatty looked under the bed to see if anyone was hiding there. No—there were only cardboard boxes and rubbish of all kinds.

The little dog suddenly ran in and put her tiny paws on his leg. Fatty petted her and she wagged her tail. The woman called her. 'Poppet!' and the poodle rushed out again. Fatty went into the third room, an untidy kitchen, with a miserable little larder. There was not much in it, and it was very dirty.

'What a place!' thought Fatty. 'Certainly the Lorenzos are not being hidden by the Larkins—and anyway they'd never be able to endure hiding in a filthy little hole like this. Pooh—it smells!'

He looked at the ceilings of the three rooms, wondering if there might be an attic or boxroom up above. There was no trap-door, no opening of any kind. The Lorenzos were definitely not there—so that was that, thought Fatty!

The woman appeared at the little front door. 'Ain't you finished yet?' she said, her harsh voice grating unpleasantly on Fatty's ears. She sniffed and pulled her old shawl tightly round her.

'Yes. Just going,' said Fatty briskly, snapping the elastic round the card and the board he carried. 'Bit of a job to find the meter. Well, so-long!'

He stepped out into the little garden. Then he looked back suddenly. 'Can I get into Tally-Ho House to read the meters?' he asked. 'I did hear as the folk had done a bunk. Did you know them?'

'It's none of your business,' said the woman sullenly. She sniffed again and shut the door. Poppet had gone in with her.

'Well—I've learnt something definite—and that is that the Lorenzos are certainly not being hidden in that cottage!' he thought, as he made his way to the wicket-gate.

He found Ern just outside, waiting for him. Ern had done his job of watching and whistling and now wanted to join up with the others again. He stared hard at Fatty.

'Lovaduck! You don't half look queer with that moustache, Fatty,' he said. 'Did you find out anything?'

'Only that the Lorenzos are definitely not there,' said Fatty. 'And we also decided that no car had been to the house last night, Ern, because the gates are nailed together with wooden bars.'

'Oh,' said Ern. 'It couldn't have been a car I heard then.'

'Ern—do you think the splashing noise you heard could have been *oars*?' asked Fatty, as they walked along to the boat-house.

'Oars? Well, yes—they might have been,' said Ern. He watched a boat coming up the river and nodded his head. 'Yes, of course! The noise those oars make is exactly like the splish-splash noise I heard.'

'Good! I didn't think it could be swans,' said Fatty. 'They swim so silently. Well, we think now that perhaps last night's visitors came by *boat*!'

'By boat! Where from?' said Ern, startled.

'We don't know—we haven't thought yet,' said Fatty. He hailed the others as they came up to the boat-house. 'Here's Ern—and he thinks those splashes he heard *were* made by the oars of a boat!'

'Oh—it's you, Fatty!' said Bets, looking out of the boat-house door. 'Any news? You don't look very excited!'

'I'm not,' said Fatty and went into the boat-house, where the others were waiting with Buster. 'I went to read the meter—which I couldn't find, by the way; and there are only three rooms in the place. There was absolutely no sign of the Lorenzos there. I only saw that awful woman with the wig and the sniffs. I must say she looks jolly ill.'

'Oh. Then we're all wrong again,' said Larry, in disappointment. 'The Lorenzos *aren't* hiding here! Now we've got to think of something else. Do you suppose they just came and went away again—without even taking Poppet?'

'Let's get into the boat and talk,' said Fatty. 'We're nice and private in this boat-house.'

They all got into the little boat and let it bob under them up and down, up and down, as the waves ran in and out.

'What I can't understand now is why the Lorenzos *came* last night—if it was them—talked to the Larkins, and then went away again,' said Fatty. 'And where did they come from, in the boat? They must have taken a boat from the opposite bank—or from somewhere further up or down the river . . .'

'Maidenhead!' said Bets, at once.

'Why yes, of course—*Maidenhead*!' said Fatty, at once. 'What an ass I am! Of *course*—that's why they *went* to Maidenhead—so that they could come here by river.'

'Jolly long way to row,' said Larry. 'Miles!'

'Did they come by motor-boat?' wondered Fatty—and immediately got a clap on the back from Ern.

'You've got it, Fatty! You've got it! *That* was the noise I heard last night! Not a car—nor an aeroplane—but a motor-boat!'

The boat rocked with Ern's excitement! Fatty sat up straight. 'Yes, Ern! That's what you heard! And the oars you heard splashing were the oars of *this* boat going out in mid-stream to the motor-launch! She couldn't come close in here because the water's much too shallow!'

'WHO took this boat out to the launch?' said Larry at once. There was a pause as all the children sorted out these new ideas.

'There must be somebody here who took out the rowing-boat and brought one or both of the Lorenzos back in it,' said Pip. 'And then probably took them back to the motor-launch again, as they're not hiding here after all.'

'Then, if that's so, the only thing they could have come for would be to bring the picture here to hide!' said Fatty.

'Yes! And if it was Mrs. Lorenzo, she came to see her little poodle too,' said Bets.

'I think you're right, Bets,' said Fatty. 'Certainly the

120

poodle seems much happier now—and her little tail was wagging like anything. Just as if she had seen her mistress —and her master too, probably—and felt that they hadn't really deserted her.'

'I'm sure we're right,' said Daisy, in excitement. 'We've reasoned it all out jolly well! The Lorenzos went to Maidenhead in order to get here by boat. They came by motor-boat—and old Larkin met them in this rowing-boat. He rowed them back here to the bank—helped them to carry the crated picture to shore—took Mrs. Lorenzo to see her precious dog . . .'

'Yes! That's when I heard the talking and the barking!' said Ern, almost upsetting the boat in his excitement.

'And then when the picture was put in some safe hiding-place, old Larkin rowed them out to the motor-boat again, rowed himself back here and put the boat in this boat-house—and went to bed,' finished Fatty, triumphantly.

'We've solved the mystery!' said Ern, thrilled. The others laughed.

'Indeed we haven't, Ern,' said Fatty. 'We still don't know the two important things—where the Lorenzos are —and where the picture is!'

'Sright!' said Ern, his excitement fading.

'We really ought to have a JOLLY GOOD LOOK for that hidden picture,' said Pip. 'We *know* it was brought here last night—at least, we're pretty sure—so it must be some-where in the grounds. A big crate wouldn't easily be hidden. It's in some out-house or somewhere like that. It might even be buried.'

'It's too late to look for it now,' said Fatty, looking at his watch.

'Oh, Fatty—just let's have a *quick* look round,' begged Bets. 'We could easily pop our heads into the green-houses and out-houses.'

'All right,' said Fatty. 'Let's get out of this boat then. Be CAREFUL, Ern—you nearly upset us all, leaping out like that!'

'I say—here's something at the bottom of the boat,' said

Bets, 'something bright.' She bent down to get it. 'Oh—it's only a nice new drawing-pin, look!'

Fatty took it and stared at it. 'I bet I know where *that* came from!' he said, in excitement. 'From the crate the picture was in! I bet this was one of the pins that pinned the label to the crate—big crates usually have labels fastened on with drawing-pins. This is a good find, Bets—it's certain now that the picture and its crate were in this boat last night.'

'Come on, quickly! Let's find it!' cried Pip, and he too almost upset the boat as he leapt out. Everyone felt suddenly excited again.

'It's a clue!' said Bets, taking the pin from Fatty. 'Isn't it, Fatty? Our first real clue!'

Fatty laughed. 'I hope so. Come on, Buster—keep to heel.'

They all left the boat-house and went back to the wicket-gate. They looked to see if the Larkins were anywhere about. There was a light already in the little cottage and the six felt sure that the old man and his wife were safely indoors.

They slipped silently into the grounds. Pip stopped and pointed over to a distant corner. 'What's that?' he said. 'It's a bonfire, isn't it? Let's go and see it. I could do with a bit of warmth!'

They were soon standing round the bonfire, which was roaring up as if it had had paraffin put on it. Bets gave a sudden exclamation, and bent down to pick something up. 'Fatty! Look—another drawing-pin just like the other one. The crate must be somewhere here!'

A LITTLE BIT OF FUN

FATTY looked at the pin and compared it with the first one. Yes—they were exactly the same. Then he looked closely at the roaring flames. He picked up a fallen branch of dead wood and poked the fire, raking out what was in it.

'Look!' he said. 'Here's the crate! It's burning in the fire! It's been chopped up well, and thrown here—and then set alight so that no sign may be left of it!'

The children stared as Fatty pointed out bits of wood that had obviously come from a cheap crate. 'Here's a fragment of a label,' said Larry, pouncing on a burning piece of thick paper. He blew out the flames. Only three letters still showed on the paper.

'n-h-e,' said Larry. 'That's all that's left, I'm afraid.'

'It's enough,' said Fatty, at once. 'It tells us where the crate comes from—where it was last sent to be picked up by the Lorenzos! "n-h-e" are the sixth, seventh and eighth letters of the word Maidenhead! Count and see!'

'Gosh yes!' said Pip. 'You're jolly sharp, Fatty. Well, I suppose the picture's gone now—burnt with the crate, so that no one can discover it.'

'Don't be an ass,' said Fatty. 'The picture has been

unpacked and hidden—and the crate has been burnt to destroy all signs of it. It would be easy to hide just a painting. I expect it was cut neatly out of its frame—and then the frame and crate burnt together. There's some funny golden-looking stuff here and there in the fire—I bet that's all that is left of the lovely frame.'

The fire was still blazing, for the crate had been quite big. The children left it, certain that there was nothing more to be learnt there.

'We're getting warm!' said Fatty, as they walked away. 'We know now that the picture we have to look for is no longer in a big crate, nor even in a frame. It's probably just a rolled-up bit of canvas!'

'Yes. That would be *much* easier to hide!' said Daisy. 'It's probably in the Larkins' house.'

'I don't think so,' said Fatty. 'The Lorenzos wouldn't give the picture itself into the care of those dirty old Larkins! They might easily ruin it. No—it's put in a very safe place—but not in that cottage!'

They went out of the wicket-gate and took their bicycles. They were just about to walk them down the path to the river-road when Fatty pulled them back.

'Look out! There's Goon!' he said. And, sure enough, skulking in the shadows not very far in front of them was the familiar figure of Mr. Goon!

'What's he doing?' whispered Fatty. 'He's following someone, isn't he?'

'Yes—there's a man some way ahead of him, carrying a bag of some kind,' whispered Larry. 'Who is it?'

'I don't know. But we'll soon find out,' said Fatty briskly. 'As soon as we get to the road, and can ride our bikes, get on them and ride right up to Goon, ringing your bells madly, just to tell him we're here—and then ride on as fast as you can to see who he's following. I've no idea who it can be—but we ought to find out if Goon has got some kind of a Suspect he's trailing!'

They leapt on their bicycles as soon as they reached

the road and raced after Mr. Goon, who was still hugging the shadows. It was getting dark now and the children had switched on their lamps. They made quite a bright light on the road. As they overtook Mr. Goon he crouched back into the shadows, not wanting to be seen.

'Jingle-jingle-rrrrrr-ing, tinga-linga-long!' went the bells as they raced past him.

'Night, Mr. Goon!' yelled Fatty. 'Pleasant walk to you!'

'Good night, good night, Mr. Goon,' shouted everyone, and Ern boldly yelled, 'Night, Uncle!' as he raced past, almost deafening Goon with his very loud bell.

'Gah!' said Mr. Goon in angry disgust. Now they had warned the man he was trailing—yes, he had shot off into a nearby wood. He'd never find him again! Gah!

The six bicyclists saw the man quite clearly. It was Mr. Larkin, with a shopping bag over his arm, shuffling along, his back bent and his head poked forward. His old cap was down over his nose as usual. He went into a little thicket of trees and disappeared.

'He must have been going shopping,' said Bets. 'Why is Goon trailing him? Perhaps he thinks he may lead him to some Clue!'

'Probably,' said Fatty. 'Well, he'll find it difficult to trail old Larkin now. How I'd love to lead Goon a good old dance if he followed *me*!'

'Yes! You'd have him panting and puffing!' said Pip. 'You'd better disguise yourself as Larkin, and have some fun with Goon!'

Fatty laughed. 'I've a jolly good mind to! I really have! It would serve Goon right for telling that frightful fib about me to the Superintendent—saying I'd locked him up in the boiler-house—and Johns too. I don't suppose either of them even *heard* the door being locked. I bet they were snoring too loudly.'

'Oh, Fatty—will you *really* dress up as Larkin? When?' asked Bets. 'Please, please show us yourself if you do.'

'All right,' said Fatty, feeling very drawn to the idea of

giving Goon a slight punishment for his untruthful tale to the Chief. 'I'll have my tea and then I'll have a shot at it. I only hope Goon won't retire to bed for the evening, seeing that he had a late night last night! I'd dearly love to lead him round the town!'

'Don't forget to come and see us first!' called Bets, as they parted at the cross-roads. Fatty grinned to himself as he rode on. Yes—he'd certainly like to have a bit of fun with Goon!

Fatty had a very good tea indeed. He had it by himself because his mother was out, and the cook, who completely spoilt him, piled his tray with all the things he liked best. By the time he had finished Fatty didn't feel very like having a bit of fun with anyone!

'Well—at any rate I'm fat enough to masquerade as the plump Mr. Larkin!' he thought, looking at himself in the long mirror down in his shed. 'Now then—let's sort out a few Larkin-like clothes.'

He went rapidly through his enormous collection of clothes, pulling out drawer after drawer of the big old chest. 'Ah—baggy trousers, stained and messy. Good. Old boots. Frightful old overcoat—my very worst one!'

He pulled out a coat that had long since been discarded by the last-but-one gardener the Trottevilles had had. Just right!

'Scarf—dirty grey and raggedy. This will do.' He shut his eyes for a moment and pictured old Bob Larkin clearly in his mind. Fatty had a wonderful gift for clear observation, and he could see the old fellow almost as if he were there before him.

'Nasty little unkempt beard—straggly moustache— shaggy eyebrows—glasses with thick lenses—and a horrible cap with a peak pulled sideways over his face. Yes—I can do all that!'

Fatty worked quickly and happily. First of all he made up his face and changed it utterly. Wrinkles appeared, and shaggy eyebrows over eyes almost hidden under thick glasses. A straggly moustache, a tooth gone in front (Fatty blacked one out!) and a beard that he trimmed to resemble Mr. Larkin's—thin and untidy. He glued it to his chin and looked at himself in the glass.

'You horrid old fellow!' said Fatty to his reflection. 'You nasty bit of work! Ugh! I don't like you a bit! Put on your scarf and cap!'

On went the scarf, and then the cap at exactly the right angle. Fatty grinned at himself. He was old Larkin to the life!

'I hope to goodness I don't meet Mother coming in or she'll scream the place down!' said Fatty. 'Now, Buster, I regret to say I can't take you with me tonight—and in any case a self-respecting, well-brought-up dog like you wouldn't want to be seen out with an old rogue like me!'

Buster didn't agree. He didn't mind *how* Fatty looked —he was always his dearly-beloved master!

Fatty shut Buster up and made his way cautiously to the road. It was dark now and no one was about. Fatty took his bicycle and rode to Pip's. He gave their special whistle and Pip came flying down to the garden.

'Is it you, Fatty? I'm longing to see you. Larry and Daisy are here—and Ern's come along too. I can't see you here, it's too dark—it's quite safe to come up because Mother's got a bridge party on. Don't make a noise, that's all.'

Fatty went up to the playroom. Pip flung the door open and Fatty went in, bent and stooping, shuffling along with a half-limp just like old Larkin.

Bets gave a little scream. 'Oh no—it's not Fatty. It's Mr. Larkin himself. Fatty's sent him in to trick us!'

'Lovaduck!' said Ern, startled.

'Marvellous, Fatty, marvellous!' cried Larry, and clapped him on the back.

Fatty gave a horrible hollow cough, and then cleared his throat as he had heard Larkin do. He spoke in a cracked old voice.

"'Ere! Don't you slap the stuffing out of me like that, young feller! I'll have the police on you, straight I will. Yus—I'll call in me old pal, Mr. Goon!'

They all roared with laughter. 'It's the best you've ever done, Fatty, quite the best. Oh, can't we come with you?'

'No,' said Fatty, straightening up and speaking in his own voice. 'For all we know I shan't find Goon wandering about on the watch for me, thinking I'm Larkin—he'll probably be in his armchair, snoozing over a pipe.'

'You'd better go now,' said Pip urgently. 'I can hear Mother bustling about. She's probably coming up here to fetch something. Go, Fatty—and jolly good luck. You look simply FRIGHTFUL!'

Fatty went downstairs cautiously, and crept to the garden door just as Mrs. Hilton came along to go up the stairs. He found the big black cat outside the garden door, waiting to come in, and gave her such a shock that she leapt into the night with a howl!

Fatty mounted his bicycle and rode off to Goon's. He saw a light in Goon's front window and looked in. Yes—Goon was there, looking through some letters. Fatty decided to give him a fright.

He went up to the window, and pressed his face against it. Then he coughed his hollow cough. Mr. Goon looked up at once, and gaped when he saw what he thought to be the face of old Larkin at his window.

'Hey, you!' cried Mr. Goon. 'I want to speak to you! Hey!' He grabbed his helmet, put it on and rushed out.

Fatty hurried away, and then began to walk like old Larkin, shuffle-limp, shuffle-limp. Goon saw him in the distance and paused. Oho—so old Larkin had been spying on him through the window, had he? Well, he, Goon, would have another try at stalking him. Where was he going to at this time of night? Goon felt very, very suspicious of Mr. Larkin!

'Peering in at me like that! Must be mad! He knows more than he's said he does,' thought Goon to himself, and set off after the supposed Mr. Larkin, keeping well to the shadows.

Fatty chuckled. 'Come on, Mr. Goon! I'll take you for a lovely walk! Do you good to take off some of your weight. Come along!'

F

A GOOD DEAL HAPPENS

Goon followed Fatty as closely as he dared. Fatty, looking back every now and again, decided to lead Goon to an allotment, where there were a few sheds. He could look into each one and make Goon wonder what he was doing.

He went as quickly as he could, shuffle-limp, shuffle-limp, and Goon marvelled that old Larkin could get along so quickly with his bad leg. Fatty, having a quick look round, also marvelled that big, burly Goon managed to hide himself so well in the dark shadows. Goon was really quite clever sometimes!

He came to the allotments, and Goon took a loud hissing breath! Oho! He was after tools or something, was he? That Larkin! He never had liked him, and now that he was mixed up in this Lorenzo case Goon was even more suspicious of him. He even began to wonder if Larkin knew where the stolen picture was!

Fatty enjoyed himself. He examined sheds and even bent down to pick some grass, which Goon immediately noted. 'Ah—what's he picking now? Brussels sprouts, I'll be bound! The rascal!'

Fatty left the allotments and went into the children's playground not far off. Goon, standing behind a tree, watched him suspiciously. Now what was old Larkin going into the playground for? Something queer, anyway!

To his great astonishment Fatty went to one of the

swings and sat down. He began to swing to and fro watching the amazed Goon out of the corner of his eye.

'Look at that!' said the mystified Goon to himself. 'He must be daft—quite daft. Coming here at night to have a swing! Ah—he's off again. I wouldn't be surprised if he's not on the look-out for a little burglary!'

Fatty slipped out of the playground chuckling. He went into the well-lighted main street. There someone stopped him.

'Well, Bob Larkin! Haven't seen you for some time! Come and have a bite with me and my missus!'

Fatty looked at the speaker—a tall thin man with a drooping moustache. He answered in Larkin's quavering old voice.

'I'm not too bad! Can't stop just now, though. Got some business to do!' And off he went, shuffle-limp, shuffle-limp. Goon loomed up out of the shadows. Who was that that Larkin had spoken to? Had he come out to meet anyone—someone sent by the Lorenzos, perhaps? Dark suspicions began to form in Mr. Goon's mind. What was old Bob Larkin Up To?

Fatty took him back to the playground again and had another swing. By this time Goon didn't know whether to think that Larkin was completely mad, or was waiting about to meet somebody—and filling in his time with a few odd things such as having a swing.

He decided to tackle old Larkin. This wasn't funny any more—hanging about under bushes and trees on a cold January night, watching somebody rush up and down through the town, peep into sheds, swing to and fro . . . he'd have to find out what he was doing. So he hailed the shuffling fellow in front of him.

'Hey, you! Bob Larkin! I want to speak to you!' But the figure in front only hurried on more quickly, trying to keep under the dark trees. Goon became much more suspicious.

'Why doesn't he stop when he's told to! He knows my voice all right! HEY! BOB LARKIN!'

On went Fatty, grinning to himself. Come on, Goon—a nice long walk will do you all the good in the world. Where shall we go now?

Fatty thought that a really good finish would be to take Goon right back to Larkin's cottage! He could easily disappear somewhere there, and Goon would think that old Larkin had gone into his little house. Fatty chuckled.

Goon soon realized that Larkin was off home, and he began to run. To his enormous surprise, the figure in front began to run too! Gone was the limp, gone was the shuffle! Goon couldn't believe his eyes.

Down to the river—along the river-path—through the little wicket-gate—up the path to Larkin's cottage which stood under the shadow of the tall tree in which was Ern's tree-house.

Goon panted after Fatty. Slam, went the gate and up the path came Goon, full of rage. He'd teach old Larkin to lead him a dance like this, and not answer when he was shouted at!

Fatty hid in a bush, and watched Mr. Goon stride up to the little cottage. He knocked so fiercely on it with his knuckles that he almost scraped the skin off. The door opened cautiously, and Bob Larkin's head appeared in the crack, gazing at Goon's angry face in amazement.

'Now then, you!' said Goon angrily, 'what's the meaning of all this?'

'All what?' said Larkin.

Goon snorted. It was one of his very best snorts. 'Gah! Don't try and put it across me that you don't know what you've just been doing. Leading me such a dance—swinging in the playground . . .'

Larkin looked more and more amazed. He called back over his shoulder to Mrs. Larkin. 'I haven't set foot out of doors tonight, have I?'

'No,' came back the answer, followed by a sniff and a cough.

'There you are!' said Larkin. 'You've made a silly mistake.' He tried to shut the door but Mr. Goon put his big foot in to prevent him.

'You mean to tell me you haven't been trotting in front of me this last hour?' he panted in rage. 'You mean to tell me you didn't snoop in them allotment sheds to see what you could take—and . . .'

'You're mad!' said Mr. Larkin, really alarmed now.

'What were you out for tonight?' asked Mr. Goon. 'That's what I want to know. You'll be sorry for this, Larkin. Obstructing the Law, that's what you're doing. And you can be put in prison for that, and well you know it. Where's me notebook?'

He took his foot out of the door for half a moment and quick as lightning Mr. Larkin crashed it shut. There was the sound of a key turning in the lock.

Fatty began to laugh. He had been bottling it up, but now he couldn't hold it in any longer. Afraid that Mr. Goon would hear him, he made his way to the back of the cottage, his handkerchief over his mouth. He stood there, shaking with mirth, thinking of old Larkin's amazement, and Goon's fury. Oh, what a night!

After a while he quietened down. Where was Goon? There wasn't a sound of him now. He must have gone home in rage, to write out a report of the night's doings. How queer it would sound!

Fatty decided to wait a minute or two, in case Goon hadn't gone. He sat down on an old box, looking exactly like a poor, tired old man!

Then things began to happen again. The back door suddenly opened, and a beam of light shone right on the surprised Fatty. Mrs. Larkin stood there with some rubbish in her hand to put into the dustbin, and she saw Fatty clearly. She put her hand up to her mouth, and a look of real terror came over her white face. She rushed screaming indoors.

Fatty got up at once, suddenly sobered. He hadn't meant to frighten anyone—but, of course, Mrs. Larkin must have been completely amazed to see him sitting there.

'She leaves her husband sitting indoors—opens the back door and apparently sees him sitting outside too!' thought Fatty. 'No wonder she screamed. A husband behind her, and a husband in front of her—not too good!'

Fatty crept away to the Woosh's garden, which was very near the back of the Larkins' cottage. He didn't want to risk being seen by Mrs. Larkin again—she would probably faint with fright, poor thing!

He was just squeezing through the hedge into the Woosh's garden, when he heard someone coming out of the Larkins' back door, someone speaking in an urgent whisper, though Fatty could not hear what was said.

He wished he hadn't chosen such a thick piece of the hedge—blow it, he couldn't get through! Then somebody came right up to the hedge, and caught hold of him. Fatty caught the glint of glasses, and saw that it was old Larkin himself. Now what was he to do!

He shook off the man's hand and with one great heave, fell into the garden next door. The voice came urgently again. 'How did you get back? What have you come for?'

But Fatty did not wait to answer. He fled.

He ran to the Woosh's gate and slipped out of it—only to hear a familiar voice say, 'Ah! I *thought* you'd be out and about again, Bob Larkin! You *are* up to some mischief tonight, aren't you! You come alonga me!'

Goon was standing in the shelter of some bushes, and he made a grab at Fatty's arm as he passed. Fatty had a terrible shock! He pulled away, and heard his coat ripping. But he was off like a hare, with Goon after him. Where now?

The wicket-gate of the Larkins' had been left open—and Fatty dashed back through it. He could easily hide somewhere in the grounds. Goon panted after him—and just then, round the corner of the cottage, attracted by the noise, came Bob Larkin himself, having found it impossible to get through the hedge after Fatty.

Fatty ran full-tilt into him, and they both fell over. Goon

134

To his enormous astonishment he saw two Mr. Larkins.

came up, and shone his lamp downwards in glee. Ah—now he'd got that fellow all right!

To his enormous astonishment he saw *two* Mr. Larkins on the ground. Two faces with straggly beards and shaggy eyebrows and thick glasses looked up at him, blinking in the light of the lantern.

'Ow!' said Goon, his hand beginning to shake. ''Ere—what's all this? I don't like it! I . . . I . . . d-d-don't li . . .'

Poor Goon couldn't bear it any longer. He turned and ran down the path as if a dozen Mr. Larkins were after him. He made a peculiar moaning sound as he went, and if Fatty hadn't had all the wind knocked out of him by the collision with Larkin, he would have laughed loudly.

'Now,' said Mr. Larkin, in a peculiarly unpleasant voice, 'now, just you . . .'

But Fatty was off again, and away into the darkness. He made for Tally-Ho House. There were many corners there to hide in if Larkin came after him.

But he heard no more sound from Larkin. He stood for a while near the boiler-house, listening, but could hear nothing at all. Fatty gave a little sigh. What an evening! He thought it would be just as well to go home again now —he really felt astonishingly tired!

He cautiously left his hiding-place and made his way round the house. It was very dark there, with high trees all round, overshadowing the house. Fatty didn't dare to put on his torch, for fear of being spotted, so he stepped forward slowly and carefully.

He bumped his head into something hard, and stopped. What was this? He put out his hand and took hold of something. It felt like a long pole of wood, slanting upwards—and wait, there was more—gosh, of course—it was a ladder! A ladder leading up to the balcony. Wheeeew! What was this now?

Fatty went up the ladder! It led to the balcony rails. Fatty cautiously climbed over the rails and felt about for the door. Was someone inside the house?

But the door wouldn't open. It was locked. Fatty

remembered what the Superintendent had told him—all doors were bolted on the inside except the garden door, which had had a special lock put on it so that only the police could get in and out.

Who put the ladder there then? An ordinary burglar? Was he still waiting about in the shadows, furious with Fatty for discovering his ladder?

Fatty was suddenly overcome with panic, and slid down the ladder at top speed. He tore off to the wicket-gate, seeing Goons and Larkins and burglars in every shadow! It wasn't till he was safely in the very middle of a well-lighted road that he calmed down, and felt ashamed of himself—gosh, he didn't often feel scared! Whatever had come over him?

MORE PUZZLES

ABOUT HALF AN HOUR later Fatty sat in a hot bath and thought over the extraordinary evening. It needed a little sorting out!

First of all, should he ring up the Chief and tell him about the ladder? No—he might have to explain his mad idea of disguising himself as Larkin and leading Goon such a dance. Fatty felt that the Chief might not see the funny side of that. He wondered if Goon would make a report on the evening. How would he explain two Larkins?

Then that ladder. Fatty was inclined to think that the thief had been up it, tried the door and given up the idea of getting in when he found it was both locked *and* bolted. In any case it would take a bold burglar to come back again after he had heard all the shouting and scrimmaging that had been going on. Fatty felt sure that if the burglar *had* been anywhere about, he would certainly have gone while the going was good!

He was sorry he had frightened Mrs. Larkin. Then he remembered Goon's face of horror when he shone his lantern down and saw *two* Mr. Larkins on the ground looking up at him. *Two!* He must have thought he was seeing double! Fatty grinned, and began to soap himself thoroughly.

He thought about Mr. Larkin. What was it that he had

said to Fatty when he first saw him? Fatty frowned and tried to remember. It was something like 'How did you get back? What have you come for?'

It seemed a funny thing to say—unless Larkin imagined he was Lorenzo. He probably couldn't see him properly in the dark. Or more likely Fatty hadn't heard him correctly. Fatty dismissed the incident from his mind and began to worry once more about whether he ought to telephone Superintendent Jenks or not.

'No. I'll leave well alone,' thought Fatty, soaping himself all over again. 'Of course, if Goon telephones him with his tale of chasing two Bob Larkins, and the Chief puts two and two together, and jumps to the fact that one of them was me, then I shall quite likely be all set for trouble—I'll chance it. I don't think Goon *will* send in that report!'

Goon didn't. When at last he got home, in a state of fury, fright and utter bewilderment, he sat down heavily in his armchair, and stared at nothing. He forgot that he had asked the daily woman to come in and cook his dinner for him that night, and when she knocked at his door, he almost leapt from his chair in fright. He gazed at the door, half afraid that another Mr. Larkin would appear round it.

'Who—who is it?' he said, in husky tones.

The woman put her untidy head round the door, surprised at Goon's unusual voice. 'Only me, sir. About your dinner.'

'Ah,' said Goon, in a more ordinary voice. 'Yes. Yes, bring it in.'

The evening's mishaps had not spoilt Goon's appetite. He thought hard as he ate his stew, and gradually recovered from his fright. He jabbed at a bit of meat.

'*Two* Larkins. Sure as I'm here, there were two. But what will the Chief say if I send in a report and say I saw *two*? "My dear Goon," he'll say, "you must have been seeing double. Hadn't you better buy yourself some glasses?"'

Goon mimicked the Chief's voice, and felt very pleased with his imitation. 'Ho, Chief!' he said. 'Ho! Glasses I need, do I? Let me tell you this—I don't need glasses, and I don't need advice from you—all I want is a spot of promotion, which is more than due to me. . . .'

He jumped at another knock at the door, but it was only the woman again. 'Oooh—I thought you must have someone here,' she said. 'I heard talking.'

'Bring in the pudding,' said Goon loftily. Ha, *he'd* tell the Chief a few things if he had him here this very minute! But no, not about the two Larkins. On the whole it would be better to keep that to himself. Goon began to doubt whether he *had* seen two? Had he? Yes, he had. No, he hadn't. Yes—ah, here was the pudding, steaming hot, too!

Next morning Fatty sent for the others early. He had such a lot to tell them. He had got up very early himself because he had suddenly remembered that he had left his bicycle somewhere near Goon's house, and he didn't want Goon to spot it there. So, before eight o'clock Fatty had shot off to get it, and was very thankful to see that it was still there!

'Fatty! What happened last night? Did Goon see you?' asked Bets, as soon as she saw him.

Fatty nodded. He felt rather pleased with himself now. What a tale he had to tell! He began to tell it, and the others roared with laughter. As for Ern, he rolled over and over on the floor unable to stop—the thought of his fearsome uncle chasing Fatty all over the place, and even watching him on the swings was too much for him.

'Stop, Fatty! Stop a bit, and let me get over this,' begged poor Ern. 'Oooh, my sides! Fatty, stop!'

The story went on to its thrilling end. Everyone listened with the utmost attention, even Buster. When Fatty came to the bit where he had bumped into the ladder, everyone exclaimed. 'Here's the bump I got on my forehead—see?' said Fatty, displaying quite a satisfactory bump.

'Oh! I *wish* I'd been there to see all this!' said Bets.

'What did you do after you had come down the ladder, Fatty?'

'Oh—I just went home and had a bath,' said Fatty, deciding that he needn't spoil this thrilling tale by relating how he had scuttled back home at top speed!

'A very interesting evening!' said Pip. 'But it doesn't seem to get us much farther, Fatty, does it? Do you plan for us to do anything this morning?'

'Well—I thought we'd go and see if the ladder is still there,' said Fatty. 'We might find footprints or something at the bottom—you never know.'

'I can't think why old Larkin asked you why you had come back, when he saw you,' said Larry. 'He must have thought you were Lorenzo.'

'Yes. That's what *I* thought,' said Fatty. 'If he'd seen me *properly*—looking exactly like himself, of course—he wouldn't have asked such an idiotic question. Mrs. Larkin saw me all right though—that's what gave her such a shock, I expect—leaving old Larkin behind her in the house—and seeing another Larkin outside!'

'Let's go,' said Pip, getting up. 'That was a marvellous tale, Fatty. I wish I dared do the things you do, but I daren't. And if I did they wouldn't have such fine endings as yours. I wonder what old Goon is thinking this morning?'

They all went off on their bicycles, Buster in Fatty's basket. They decided not to go in at the wicket-gate in case old Bob Larkin was in a temper because of the happenings of the night before.

They went past the gate and came to a place where they could easily get into the grounds. They left their bicycles there and made their way to the big house.

'The ladder was the other side,' said Fatty, and led the way. But as soon as they turned the corner of the house he saw that the ladder was gone.

'It's not there!' he said. 'Well—I wonder if the burglar got in after I left, then—he must have been about, because he's removed the ladder! Gosh—I wish I'd reported seeing

141

it, now—I might have prevented a burglary! I wonder if he managed to get in. Look—there are the marks made by the foot of the ladder in the ground.'

'Let's walk round the house and peep in at the windows to see if any rooms have been ransacked,' said Daisy. So they walked all round, peeping into every window. Nothing was disturbed at all, as far as they could see.

They came to the last window and peered through it. 'Ah—this is the one with the big bowl of dead flowers,' said Fatty, remembering. 'There they are still—deader than ever! And the chairs are still all in their dust-sheets.'

His eyes slid round, remembering everything—and then he frowned. Something was missing. He was sure it was. Something that had puzzled him. Yes—there had been a little rubber bone on the floor, beside that stool. But it had gone now!

Fatty peered and peered, trying to see the bone. But it had definitely gone! How puzzling!

'There's one thing missing,' said Fatty. 'A little rubber bone—a dog's plaything. It probably used to belong to Poppet the poodle. I saw it down by that stool.'

'You must be mistaken, Fatty,' said Larry. 'Nobody would steal a dog's rubber bone! Nothing seems to be disturbed at all. I don't think that burglar could have managed to get in.'

'I *did* see a rubber bone,' said Fatty. 'I don't make mistakes about a thing like that. I call that very curious. Very curious indeed.'

They left the house and wandered around a little more. Buster left them and went off by himself, having suddenly had a very good idea. He'd go and play with that nice little poodle!

So he trotted off to the cottage and barked a small and polite bark. Poppet at once leapt up to the window-ledge and looked out.

Bets heard Buster barking and ran to get him. She saw the little poodle at the window—and how Bets stared!

142

Not at Poppet—but at something she held in her mouth! She raced back to Fatty, her face scarlet with excitement.

'Fatty! Listen! Poppet's up at the window, and she's got a rubber bone in her mouth!'

Fatty whistled. They all went cautiously down the path—and sure enough, there was Poppet trying vainly to bark with the little rubber bone between her teeth.

'Yes—that's the one,' said Fatty. 'Buster, come here. Look—let's all go quietly back to our bikes and have a talk. This is important.'

They all went to their bikes, feeling suddenly excited. Fatty's eyes shone. 'It must have been the *Larkins* who went into the house last night! Nobody else would have bothered about a rubber bone. *They* had a dog, so it was an ordinary thing to do to pick it up and take it back to Poppet, and . . .'

'*I* don't think it was an ordinary thing for them to do,' said Bets. 'We know they're unkind to Poppet—we've even heard them "lamming" her, as they call it. I don't think they'd even *bother* to take her bone back to her!'

'Yet she's got it,' said Fatty. 'Well, then—who else could have taken it to her?'

'Mrs. Lorenzo might,' said Bets. 'Perhaps it was the Lorenzos who got in last night. Perhaps they were here again.'

'Yes, they might have been,' said Fatty. 'If so, that looks as if Larkin did mistake me for Lorenzo when he saw me last night and asked me why I had come back.'

'Oh—here's Poppet! She must have escaped out of the house to look for Buster!' said Bets. 'Listen—Mrs. Larkin is calling her.'

'Take her back, Bets,' said Fatty, 'and see if you can have a chat with Mrs. Larkin. Go on—*you* might be able to get something out of her!'

'All right,' said Bets, half-scared, and took little Poppet into her arms. She went up the river-path to the wicket-gate. Buster at her heels, trying his hardest to jump up and lick the little poodle's nose.

Bets went right up to the cottage. She could hear Mrs. Larkin calling 'Poppet! Poppet!' and knew she was looking for her over by the big house. Perhaps Bets would have time just to have a look at that rubber bone so that she could tell Fatty exactly what it was like.

So Bets slipped into the small cottage and looked round for the bone. She couldn't see it, but she saw a few things that made her stare!

The kitchen table was piled with tins of food—big, expensive tins! How strange! Bets tiptoed into the bedroom. On the bed, neatly folded, were spotlessly clean blankets and an eiderdown! So it *was* the Larkins then who had put that ladder up—and they *had* got in, and *had* stolen things—food—and warm coverings—and they had picked up Poppet's rubber bone and taken it back to her.

WELL! Fatty must be told this at once!

A BELL RINGS FOR FATTY

BEFORE Bets could put Poppet down and run to Fatty, there came the sound of footsteps hurrying to the door. Bets turned. It was Mrs. Larkin, in the same old red shawl, hideous wig and dark glasses.

'Oh—you've got Poppet!' she said. 'I thought she'd fallen into the river.'

She took the little poodle from Bets, and the girl watched Poppet licking the woman's face. 'You're kind to her now,' said Bets. 'You weren't at first.'

The woman put Poppet down at once. 'Now you go,' she said harshly. 'You shouldn't have walked in without permission.'

'I'm going,' said Bets. 'Is that Poppet's basket? Oh—there's her rubber bone!'

She took it out of the basket, but the woman snatched it out of her hand and gave her a rough push. Bets ran out. She was puzzled. She waited till the door was shut then she tiptoed back and peeped in at the window. The woman was putting a mat down under the dog's basket, with Poppet fussing round.

Bets made her way back to the others, still puzzled. Why did Mrs. Larkin treat Poppet differently? Perhaps the Lorenzos had promised them a lot of money if Poppet was kept happy. That must be it.

Bets told her tale to the others. 'Big, expensive tins! Nice blankets and rugs! They must have helped themselves well,' she said. 'I didn't get anything much out of the woman, though. She was cross and pushed me out.'

'Look—there's somebody going in at the wicket-gate,' said Pip. 'Oh—it's old Larkin. Been shopping, I suppose. No—he's got no basket—and anyway they're plentifully supplied with tins now. All he's got are some papers.'

Fatty looked to see. 'Quite a few papers!' he said, surprised. 'I suppose he looks through them all each day to see if there is any news of the Lorenzos. He might read at any moment that they had been caught.'

'What do we do now?' asked Pip. 'Go and telephone to the Chief? Nobody but us knows that things have been taken from the house. It beats me how the Larkins got in, because the police said they hadn't keys. I suppose they *must* have some—and knew that possibly the only door that might not be bolted would be the balcony door. And they were right.'

'Come on,' said Fatty, taking his bicycle. 'We'll telephone.'

'I'm glad that that horrid Mrs. Larkin is so much nicer to dear little Poppet,' said Bets. 'Honestly, she might be Mrs. Lorenzo the way she fusses her now. Why, she was even putting a rug down under Poppet's basket when I peeped in at the window!'

Fatty suddenly gave such a terrific wobble on his bicycle that he almost fell off. Bets looked at him in surprise.

'What's up, Fatty?' she said.

'Don't speak to me for a minute,' said Fatty in a peculiar voice. 'I'm going to get off. You ride on, all of you.'

Bets looked at him in alarm. 'Are you ill?'

'No. I've just got an idea, that's all. Something you said rang a bell in my mind. Leave me alone for a minute,' said Fatty urgently. The others, quite mystified, rode on a little way and then got off to wait for Fatty. He was standing frowning by the side of the road, still holding his bicycle, and so lost in thought that he didn't even notice Mr. Goon cycling by.

'Ho! What's the matter with *you*!' said Mr. Goon, surprised.

'Be quiet,' said Fatty. 'I'm working something out.'

Mr. Goon went purple. Telling him to be quiet indeed! 'What you working out?' he said. 'Still worrying about them Lorenzos! They're in America or somewhere by now —so's the picture. You'll see! You just work out how to behave yourself and learn a few manners!'

Buster suddenly appeared out of the nearby hedge and flew at Mr. Goon's ankles barking delightedly. The big policeman hurriedly mounted his bicycle, and rode off, kicking out at Buster as he went.

Not even that disturbed Fatty. Goodness, what *could* he be thinking of?

'The great brain's working overtime,' said Pip. 'What *can* have struck him so suddenly?'

'He'll come along and say he's solved everything in a minute,' said Ern. 'You see if he doesn't. He's a wonder, he is!'

Fatty mounted his bicycle again, and came sailing up, looking extremely happy.

'I've got it,' he said. 'I've solved the whole thing! All tied up neatly, ready to lay at the Superintendent's feet! My word, I've been a mutt. So have we all!'

'I told you so!' said Ern triumphantly, looking round at the others. 'I said he was solving everything, didn't I, Bets?'

'But—what have you solved?' said Pip. 'Not *every*thing, surely!'

'I think so. I'm just not quite certain about one thing,' said Fatty. 'However, we'll soon know!'

'Tell us,' begged Larry. 'It's frightful, not knowing what you're talking about! Do tell us.'

'No time,' said Fatty, riding fast. 'I must get to a telephone box immediately. Buck up, all of you!'

Everyone rode behind Fatty in a terrific state of excitement. Fatty pedalled furiously, as if he was in a race. Poor old Buster was left far behind, and Bets felt very sorry for him, but even she felt that she could slow down and pick him up. Buster was most surprised at everyone's hardheartedness!

Fatty leapt off his bicycle at the nearest telephone kiosk. He dashed in, shut the door, and gave a number. The others congregated outside in wonder.

An answer came at once. 'Police here.'

'I want to speak to the Superintendent, please,' said Fatty. 'Tell him it's Frederick Trotteville here, and I've something urgent to say.'

'Right,' said the voice. In a second or two the Superintendent's crisp voice came over the wire.

'Yes? What is it, Frederick?'

'Sir, can you possibly come over here at once?' said Fatty. 'I've got everything tied up nicely for you!'

'What do you mean?' said the Chief. 'You don't mean the Lorenzo case, surely?'

'Yes, sir. I know everything!' said Fatty exultantly. 'I suddenly tumbled to it this morning. It's too long to tell you over the phone, sir. Can you come over at once—before things go wrong?'

'You're talking in riddles, Frederick,' said the Chief. 'But I'd better trust you, I suppose. I'll get the car and come at once. Where shall I find you?'

'Up by the Larkins' cottage, sir,' said Fatty. 'Do you know where it is?'

'Yes,' said the Chief. 'I'll be there.' He rang off, and Fatty put back the receiver, his face glowing. He rubbed his hands in glee before he stepped out of the kiosk.

'Fatty! You *might* tell us what's up,' said Pip. 'It's too bad—seeing you shouting into that phone and not hearing a word you were saying—and then you rub your hands in glee when you've finished. Whatever has happened so suddenly?'

'Tell you as soon as I can,' said Fatty, wheeling his bicycle into the road. 'Come on—we've got to go back to the wicket-gate leading to the Larkins' cottage. The Chief will be there as soon as possible.'

'Gosh—so that's who you've been ringing up!' said Larry, cycling madly after Fatty. 'Is he really coming over?'

'Yes—at once,' said Fatty. 'Hallo—where's Buster?'

'We've left him all behind again,' panted Bets. 'He's so miserable. Oh Fatty, do stop and pick him up.'

Fatty stopped. Buster came up at a valiant trot, his tongue hanging out almost to the ground. Fatty picked him up. 'My Poppet!' he said ridiculously, and put him into his bicycle basket. Buster heaved a great sigh of relief.

They set off again, and came to the river-path, where they had to get off and wheel their bicycles. Ern called to Fatty. 'Can't you tell us now, Fatty?'

'Too many people about,' said Fatty aggravatingly. 'Hallo, who are these?'

Two small girls had just rushed out of a nearby gate and flung themselves on Ern.

'Ern! Come and play with us! Mum's given us a picnic dinner to eat up in the tree-house. '

'Sorry,' said Ern, shaking them off. 'I've got Important Business to do, Liz and Glad. Er—these are my two cousins, Fatty—Liz, or Elizabeth. And Glad. Glad, what's *your* name short for? I never did know.'

'Gladys!' said Glad, with a giggle. 'Ern, we kept watch up in the tree-house as usual this morning, but we only saw Mr. Larkin once—he's just come in—and Mrs. Larkin once. She hung an old rug out on the line, and she's beating it.'

'All right, all right,' said Ern, while all the others looked on, amused. 'They sit up in the tree-house for me and keep their eyes open,' he explained to Fatty. He turned back to Liz and Glad.

'You go back,' he said. 'I *might* come and have dinner with you in the tree-house. Buzz off, now! I'm busy.'

They buzzed off, two skinny little things, delighted that Ern was going to have dinner with them.

'Better not gather round the wicket-gate all in a bunch,' said Fatty, in a low voice, when they got there. 'Let's go up the river-path a little way. Hallo, who's this coming?'

It was Mr. Goon, on his way to tell Mr. Larkin what he thought of him for leading him such a dance the night before. Goon had decided that he hadn't really seen two Mr. Larkins—he was so tired he must have seen double—that was what it was—and Mr. Larkin was going to hear what he thought of old men who went on the swings in the playground at dark of night. Ho!

Goon saw the children further up the path and scowled. 'You clear orf!' he called to them. 'And keep hold of that there dog! What you doing here, crowding up the pathway?'

'We're waiting for someone,' said Fatty calmly.

'Ho yes!' said Mr. Goon rudely. 'And who may you be waiting for, I'd like to know? Your friend the Superintendent perhaps? You just clear orf!'

'Actually yes, we *are* waiting for him,' said Fatty. 'That was a clever guess of yours, Goon.'

"Now don't you try to stuff me up with your Superintendent Jenks!' said Good, most sarcastically. 'He's miles from here. That I do know, for he telephoned me himself this morning.'

'Well, *you* don't need to wait and see him,' said Fatty. 'He's coming to see *us*, actually!'

Mr. Goon went slowly purple. 'Telling me fairy-tales like that!' he said. 'You clear orf, I say.'

There came the sound of a car in the distance. It stopped. A car door slammed.

'Here he is,' said Fatty to Goon, as quick footsteps came up the river-path. Goon swung round—and his mouth fell open.

It *was* Superintendent Jenks, tall and broad-shouldered as ever, followed by another man. He grinned at Fatty. 'Well.' he said, 'here I am!'

A TRULY REMARKABLE TALE!

'GOOD MORNING, SIR,' said Fatty. Goon was quite tongue-tied, and couldn't say a word. The Chief nodded to Fatty and then to Goon.

'Good morning, Frederick. Well, Goon—you here too? I didn't expect to see you as well.'

'He came along by accident,' said Fatty. 'All the others are here too, sir.'

The Chief saluted all of them solemnly and they saluted back. Ern even clicked his heels together.

'Well, now, let's get down to business,' said the Chief. 'You telephoned to say you'd got this Lorenzo business nicely tied up. Do you mean you know where the Lorenzos are?'

'Yes, sir,' said Fatty, at once, and Goon's eyes nearly fell out of his head. He stared at Fatty and swallowed hard. That boy! That Toad of a Boy. How could *he* know where the Lorenzos were?

The Chief laughed. 'Don't tell me you know where the *picture* is as well!' he said.

'I *think* I do,' said Fatty, 'but if I don't you can easily make the Lorenzos tell you.'

The Chief turned to Goon. 'I suppose you're in on this too?' he said.

151

Goon shook his head. He didn't dare to trust himself to speak.

The Chief turned back to Fatty. 'Well, where *are* the Lorenzos?' he said. 'As you've brought me over here, I imagine they're hiding in this district.'

'Yes, sir,' said Fatty. 'They're hiding in the Larkins' cottage.'

'That they're not!' burst out Goon. 'Begging your pardon, sir, but I've gone through that cottage three times —there's no one there but the two Larkins. I'm ready to swear to that.'

'Well, the Lorenzos *are* there,' said Fatty. 'Come along, Chief—I'll show you.'

He led the way, the others following in wonder. What kind of hiding-place were the Lorenzos in? It must be a very small one! Goon went along too, angry and disbelieving.

Fatty rapped at the Larkins' door. It was opened by old Larkin himself, cap on head as usual, and dirty old scarf round his throat. He peered through his thick glasses at Fatty.

'What you want?' he said. Then he saw the rest of the children and the tall Superintendent of police, and made as if to shut the door quickly. But Fatty put his foot in at once.

'We're coming in,' he said. The man that the Chief had brought with him held open the door and everyone filed in, even Buster. Mrs. Larkin was not in the room. They could hear her out in the little kitchen, rattling pans and crockery.

'What's all this?' said Larkin gruffly, in his old man's voice. 'I ain't done nuffin'.'

The little room was very crowded with so many people in it. Larkin shrank back.

'Here's *one* of the Lorenzos,' said Fatty and suddenly snatched off old Larkin's cap. Then, with a quick twist, he stripped off the man's beard, and grabbed off his shaggy eyebrows! Off came the thick glasses too! At once Larkin became a much younger man, an angry man, and a frightened one.

'Wheeeew!' whistled the Superintendent astounded. '*Bill Lorenzo!* Well, you may be a fourth-rate film-actor, but you're a first-class fraud! Masquerading as old Larkin! I saw you myself at the beginning of this case—and I could have sworn you were old Bob Larkin.'

'He wasn't Bob Larkin at *first*,' said Fatty. 'Not for some time. The real Mr. and Mrs. Larkin were here at first. Oh —here comes the other one!'

Mrs. Larkin, hearing voices, had opened the kitchen door, and stood there, staring in fright, with little Poppet in her arms. Before she could shut the door Fatty had stepped behind her.

'And here's *Mrs.* Lorenzo!' he said, and twitched off the extraordinary wig. Underneath it was pale golden hair, wavy and thick. She took off her dark glasses and looked defiantly at the surprised Chief.

'All right! I'm Gloria Lorenzo—and glad to get out of that filthy old wig of Mrs. Larkin's.' She turned to her husband. 'Bill—the game's up.'

The man nodded. It was surprising how the years fell off both of them once they had their glasses off, their own hair exposed, and stood up straight, instead of stooping. How could anyone have thought they were old and ugly?

'A marvellous disguise!' said Fatty in great admiration. 'And you both got away with it, too. Nobody had any suspicions at all that *you* were here instead of the Larkins.'

'Where *are* the Larkins?' inquired the Chief, looking all round as if they were there too.

'Bob Larkin was about last night,' said Goon. 'I saw him—*and* this fellow too.'

'What—both *together*?' said the Chief in astonishment. 'Why didn't you do something about it? Surely it must have struck you as rather odd that there should be *two* Bob Larkins?'

'One of them was *me*,' said Fatty smoothly. '*I* disguised
153

myself like old Larkin too. Sorry I led you such a dance last night, Goon—still, I had a nice swing!'

Goon almost passed out. He staggered back against the wall and put his hand in front of his eyes. So he'd been chasing *Fatty* last night not Bob Larkin—and even the other Larkin he had seen wasn't the real one. Goon began to feel extremely muddled.

'What happened to the *real* Larkins?' said the Chief. 'I really do want to know. Are they all right?'

'Well, sir, the real Larkins were left here in charge of Poppet, as you know,' said Fatty, 'and they were not kind to her at all. Then one night the Lorenzos hired a motor-launch at Maidenhead, and took it down the river. It stopped in mid-stream opposite the boat-house here . . .'

'How do you know all this?' asked Bill Lorenzo angrily. 'Has anyone split on us?'

'No,' said Fatty. He turned to the Chief. 'Ern heard noises in the night, sir, and we put two and two together, you see—about the motor-launch, I mean. Well, the *real* Bob Larkin had been warned somehow—I don't know how—to be ready that night with the rowing-boat from the boat-house. So out he went to the launch, and came back with the two Lorenzos.'

'Go on,' said the Superintendent, listening intently.

'Well, my guess is that the Lorenzos and the Larkins changed clothes,' said Fatty. 'The Lorenzos stayed behind in the cottage, and the Larkins went back to the launch and were whisked off somewhere safe—probably paid quite a bit of money, too!'

'I see, I see it all,' said the Chief, glancing at the two sullen Lorenzos. 'A very astute idea—to come back into the heart of things, where nobody would possibly be looking for them.'

'Yes—very smart, sir,' said Fatty. 'And as they are both actors, and used to making themselves up and acting all kinds of characters, it was easy to imitate the old Larkins. Er—as I have already told you, I myself imitated Larkin so successfully last night that Mr. Goon chased me all over the place!'

'It was *you* I saw here yesterday evening then!' said Bill Lorenzo. 'I thought it was old Bob Larkin himself come back again, and I couldn't understand it!'

'I know—and it was your words to me that partly helped me to understand everything,' said Fatty. 'You said—*"How did you get back? What have you come for?"* And that seemed a pretty queer thing to say to someone masquerading as *yourself*! It could only mean one thing—that you were not Bob Larkin—and therefore thought the other fellow *was*. But he was me.'

The listening Goon gave a groan. He simply couldn't follow all this. But the others could. Bets gave a little scream. 'Oh, Fatty—of course! That's why he asked you such queer questions—I never thought of that!'

'What made you *really* stumble on the whole thing?' asked the Chief. 'You'd have telephoned me last night if you had guessed then.'

'Yes, I would,' said Fatty. 'Well, lots of things gave me hints, sir. For instance, someone broke into the big house last night—and the only thing that appeared to be taken was that rubber bone on the floor there. And why should anyone take *that*? Only because they had a dog they wanted to give it to! And Bets saw tins of food on the table, and rugs and blankets on the bed—things that the Larkins wouldn't have thought of.'

'I *told* you not to take that bone!' said Bill Lorenzo angrily to his wife.

'And then we noticed that whereas at first Mrs. Larkin was very unkind to the poodle after a bit she wasn't—and the dog ran about happily all the time. That seemed queer too. And then Bets said something that rang a bell in my mind—and everything was as plain as daylight!'

'Whatever *did* I say?' said Bets, in wonder.

'You said—*"I'm glad that that horrid Mrs. Larkin is so much nicer to dear little Poppet. She might be Mrs. Lorenzo the way she fusses her now!"* And immediately I saw it all—of course, the supposed Mrs. Larkin *was* Mrs. Lorenzo—hence the fuss she made of Poppet, the taking of the tins, and the blankets for warmth—and, of course, the curious taking of such a thing as a rubber bone. It was all easy after that,' said Fatty modestly.

'Well, I'm blessed!' said the Chief. 'You've solved some things in your time, Frederick—but this beats the lot—it really does! What do you say, Goon?'

Goon said absolutely nothing at all. He was in a complete fog. He wished he was the rubber bone on the floor. He wished he was anywhere but where he was!

'You've done a remarkably fine piece of detection, Frederick,' said the Chief warmly. 'I congratulate you. What about the stolen picture? Any idea where it is? You said you weren't sure.'

The Lorenzos both stiffened, and looked quickly at Fatty.

'The Lorenzos hope I *don't* know,' said Fatty. 'They don't mind going to prison if they can hope to sell the hidden picture and get plenty of money for it when they come out! I'm not certain about the picture, sir—it's not in the crate any longer, I can tell you that. It was brought here in the boat that night, when the Lorenzos changed over with the Larkins. It was still in the crate then.'

'What happened to it?' asked the Chief.

'The picture was taken out, and the crate and frame were burnt,' said Fatty.

Bill Lorenzo gave a loud exclamation. 'How do you know all this, boy?'

'Brains, just brains,' said Fatty. He turned to the Chief. 'Now, sir, Bets happened to look in at the window here this morning, and saw Mrs. Larkin putting a rug under the poodle's basket—putting it down very carefully too. Quite a nice rug it was, too good to put under a dog's basket—and I think probably the picture has been sewn inside that rug. It's probably backed with hessian, or something—and you'll find the picture between rug and lining.'

156

'There's no rug under the dog's basket now!' said Bets, looking.

'Lovaduck! *I* know where it is!' said Ern. 'Liz and Glad told us, don't you remember?'

The Chief looked puzzled. So did everyone else. 'They're my twin cousins, sir,' said Ern. 'They've been Keeping an Eye on the Larkins for me. Well, they came rushing out to us this morning and said that they'd seen Mrs. Lorenzo hang a rug on the line, sir. I bet that's it! Nobody would ever bother to examine a rug on the line, sir! It would be a fine hiding-place—right out in the open, too! Nobody would think anything of a rug on the washing-line!'

Fatty glanced at the Lorenzos. A look of utter dismay had come over their faces. The Chief turned to his man. 'Get that rug,' he said.

They all went out of the cottage, and watched the sergeant take a rug from the washing-line. Goon stood near to Mrs. Lorenzo, and the Chief was beside Bill Lorenzo—just in case!

The rug was slit open—and inside, just as Fatty had said, was the picture, packed flat in grease-proof paper, quite unharmed.

'Phew! Fifty thousand pounds' worth of picture sewn inside a rug!' said the Chief. 'It makes me feel quite ill. Take it to the car, Sergeant.'

The Lorenzos were also taken to the car too, carefully escorted by a rather green-faced and very silent Goon, and the big Sergeant. Poppet barked a good-bye to Buster, who had been held tightly in Bets' arms all the time.

'Dear little Poppet,' said Bets, almost in tears. 'She oughtn't to belong to horrible people like that.'

'Cheer up,' said the Chief, swinging her up into the air. 'You haven't grown much, Bets! Frederick, I think this last remarkable—yes, truly remarkable feat of yours deserves a celebration! You've surpassed yourself, my boy. My word, how I shall enjoy myself when you come to work for *me*!'

'Thank you, sir,' said Fatty modestly. 'May I suggest, sir, that as it's rather cold, we all go to my shed and celebrate there? I know our cook's making mince-pies today, sir, and I've got a few things I'd like to show you—a new set of false teeth, sir, and a gadget to make large ears, and . . .'

The Chief roared. 'Large ears! Why don't you invent something in the way of large brains, Frederick—and hand a few out to poor old Goon?'

'That's an idea, sir!' said Fatty grinning, and off they all went, Ern too. What a morning!

We can't follow them, alas! The shed door is shut and there is a fine smell of mince-pies on the air. Hey, Fatty, don't wait too long for another mystery, will you!

THE END

BOOKS BY ENID BLYTON

There is no one like Enid Blyton! No other author is so popular with boys and girls as this great writer. Sales of her books run into many millions.

Have you read *all* the Enid Blyton books in Armada? If you like school stories you will want to read the Malory Towers and St. Clares' series—there are six titles in each. In her "Mystery" series (all about the Five Find-Outers and Buster the dog) thirteen exciting stories are available.

Additionally there are four Circus books and the same number of "Secret" books—wonderful value at only half-a-crown for a full-length story.

You know, Armada books are really marvellous value. The finest, biggest-selling authors appear in the Armada series, and the price is so small anyone can buy them.

Now, if you like them, why not tell your friends about them? Tell them of the thrilling stories available in Armada. Tell them of the exciting writers—Enid Blyton, Ruby Ferguson, Monica Edwards, "Biggles" and J. E. Chipperfield with his wonderful animal stories.

For a complete list of Enid Blyton's exciting stories see page 2 of this book.

ARMADA BOOKS